ROGUE VET

ROGUE VET

Melissa Moon had a feeling her kindly employer's decision to sell off his veterinary practice to a rich property company had something to do with his son Gareth Tremaine. Why else, after years of trotting round the southern hemisphere, had Gareth decided to come back? He didn't waste any time sifting through his father's finances with a fine-tooth comb either! Though Gareth's skills with the patients were inspiring she couldn't condone his ethics, and Gareth had badly miscalculated if he expected Melissa to be easy pickings too!

Rogue Vet

by

Carol Wood

Dales Large Print Books
Long Preston, North Yorkshire,
BD23 4ND, England.

British Library Cataloguing in Publication Data.

Wood, Carol
    Rogue vet.

      A catalogue record of this book is
      available from the British Library

      ISBN   978-1-84262-518-7 pbk

First published in Great Britain 1993 by Mills & Boon Limited

Copyright © Carol Wood 1993

Cover illustration © Linda Anne McKenzie

The moral right of the author has been asserted

Published in Large Print 2007 by arrangement with
Dorian Literary Agency

Dales Large Print is an imprint of Library Magna Books Ltd.

Printed and bound in Great Britain by
T.J. (International) Ltd., Cornwall, PL28 8RW

CHAPTER ONE

Melissa contemplated the green waters of the English Channel from behind the windscreen of her Mini and wished for all she was worth that her purse were as bottomless as the deep, white-tufted ocean. Just think of all she could buy! A new roof for Grampa's cottage, bedding plants for the garden and a wooden shed where his tools could be kept safely throughout the winter.

These thoughts filled her mind as with a deep sigh she drove away from the clifftops where she had parked for a few minutes in order to contemplate her woes.

'Of course you must go to London, Melissa,' her grandfather had insisted. 'And when you come home for holidays it will give us the perfect excuse for a party! I worry about you not mixing enough...'

She had left the house on a pretext of buying Sunday newspapers, but it was simply an excuse to collect her thoughts. With Gordon Tremaine's retirement from the practice and an abrupt end to her career, there seemed little hope of remaining in Dorlington. Grampa, as usual, was just making the best of things for her sake.

Melissa turned the Mini into Dorlington High Street with its familiar clusters of sea-side shops and cafeterias, slowing down at the crossroad newsagents. What happened next happened so quickly that she was never able to remember from which direction the dog actually came. He just seemed to be there, under the nose of the Mini. All she remembered was a sickening squeal of brakes and the car skewing to a halt. For a moment she simply sat still, as though the accident hadn't happened to her but to someone else. Then, with heart pounding, she felt herself fumbling for the door-handle, a sense of panic completely overtaking her.

'Is he hurt badly?' someone called as she scrambled out of the Mini.

'I ... I'm not sure,' she answered to no one in particular. Everything taking place seemed strangely unreal; the dog lying in the road, the Mini broadside-on, the elderly man hurrying towards her, alarm written all over his face. But it was when he spoke to her in such a kindly way that she seemed to wake from the inertia. 'It wasn't your fault, my dear,' she heard him say. 'I saw the dog nosing around in those litter bins over there, and then something frightened him. He ran straight out in front of you. Just lucky you were going slowly – it was only a small bump.'

Melissa knelt down and gently stroked the

dog, running her fingers through the matted hair, thinking that, small bump or not, the dog was badly dazed. 'There's a cut here on his side,' she said, finding her voice at last. 'I'm pretty sure it'll need stitching – and there may be some internal problems. Do you think you could help me get him into my car?'

The man agreed, giving her a curious glance. 'You know about animals, then?'

'I'm only a veterinary nurse, but I'll take him straight in to Mr Tremaine. The surgery isn't far away.'

She noticed that a crowd had gathered around them, but no one else offered assistance, and she was thankful that at least this one kind person was helping her. She took off her anorak and laid it on the ground. 'We shouldn't lift him any more than is necessary, so if we gently pull him with his legs trailing on to my coat and then gather up the corners to form a sort of stretcher ... like this...'

'Never fancied myself as an ambulance man, miss, but I'll give it a go!' And with a great deal of huffing and puffing the man helped her into the Mini, lowering the makeshift stretcher carefully on to the back seat. 'Phew,' he gasped, wiping his brow with a handkerchief, 'I'm not as young as I used to be!'

'Thank you for your help...' Melissa tried

to stop her teeth from chattering in spite of its being a warm late April day, guessing she was suffering from shock. 'I don't think he has any broken bones, but he's in a very neglected condition. If anyone can do anything Gordon Tremaine will, he's a marvellous vet.'

'Probably needs a lot of loving, does that poor mite.' The man peered into the back window as Melissa started the engine, and, glancing into the driving mirror, she saw he was still there as she rounded the corner.

Trying to compose herself as she drove, she ignored the silly illusion that her legs had turned into wads of cotton wool and tried to wiggle her toes just to make sure. Many times she had helped to treat animals involved in accidents, but this was the first occasion she had ever injured an animal herself, and it had to be today of all days, when she was so worried about Grampa.

'A lot of loving...' The words made her think of how lucky she was to have had her grandparents at the time of her parents' death when she was barely ten years old. Where would she be now if they hadn't looked after her? Almost certainly she would have been fostered or, even worse, sent to an institution. Instead she had been given love and security, and now when Grampa needed her support the most she had been forced to tell him she was leaving Dorlington ... it just wasn't fair!

A faint whimper came from the back seat, and Melissa glanced over her shoulder, feeling her heart melt as she looked into a pair of confused dark eyes framed by a fringe of dishevelled hair. 'It's going to be all right,' she whispered softly. 'Not much further to go now.'

Bathed in a wash of golden sunlight, the Dorset roads were thankfully quiet, and it took her less than ten minutes to arrive at the Tremaine practice. A rambling Victorian house with tall, gabled windows and billowing honeysuckle bowers, it came directly into view as she parked in the car park. Gordon Tremaine was sure to be at home, and his wife Rose would be busily baking in the kitchen in preparation for their son Gareth's arrival from Australia the following week.

Melissa soothed the dog and then hurried into the house, pushing open the heavy outer door. Quite unprepared for meeting anyone other than the Tremaines, she almost jumped out of her skin as she ran headlong into a solid barrier which proved to be a rather spectacular male chest.

'Whoa there!' The exclamation came from at least a foot above eye level. 'What's all the hurry?'

Melissa looked breathlessly up into a smiling but equally surprised face, and although she had no time to take in the features she formed the impression of a man in his early thirties following his own slow pace through the household. Had he been looking for Gordon? she wondered. If so, he would have to wait his turn today, and she determined to be polite but quite firm.

'I've an emergency, I'm afraid,' she explained, squirming past him through the inner glass doors and into the hall. 'Take a seat in Reception if you like, and I'll be with you as soon as I can...' But, disconcertingly, he began following her.

'If you're looking for the vet,' she called back to him, making it quite plain he was heading in the wrong direction, 'unless it's vitally important, I'm afraid you really are going to have to wait!'

This seemed to do the trick. He stood where he was, beamed a smile and raised his hands in a submissive gesture. Melissa congratulated herself on the small victory and hurried on into the treatment-room ... where she found precisely no one! She searched the office and the recovery-room, then picked up the phone to ring through to the kitchen. Mrs Carter the daily help was off at the weekends, and Rose Tremaine didn't seem to be at home either. There was nothing for it but to try to get the dog in by herself. Hurrying back to the car, she was horrified to find a pair of long legs protruding from the Mini. 'Just what in heaven's name do you think you're doing in my car?'

she cried, astonished at such presumption, whoever it was. 'I've got an injured animal in there – will you please get out?'

There was a muffled response from within, but the legs remained where they were. Melissa stalked around to the passenger door, yanked it open and came face to face with the stranger again. A pair of dreamy green eyes regarded her calmly.

'He's got a nasty cut there … but I don't think the muscle has been damaged. No blood from the nose or ears – you don't mind me taking a look, do you? I should really introduce myself–'

'That isn't necessary,' interrupted Melissa, not giving a hoot who he was. Fighting to push the wobbly front seat forward and losing the struggle, she saw a large hand reach out and hold it firmly back for her. 'Thank you,' she said begrudgingly, then added, to cover her harassment, 'I'm Mr Tremaine's nurse, and if you'd really like to help, you can take those two ends of the coat while I lift the other two. The sooner I get him into surgery, the better.'

'Yes, ma'am!' It was the note of sarcasm that irritated the most, and she decided at precisely that moment that there was trouble in store. Large and rugged he might be, but the smattering of knowledge he had just aired would make little odds when it came to helping practically. However, two large, suntanned hands reached out to grasp hold of the corners of her anorak, and in spite of her rising irritation Melissa found it difficult to ignore him. With a set of white teeth which caught the eye far too quickly for comfort she felt herself forced to smile back. The lean body, clad in a sporty pale blue jogging suit now quickly accruing dirty marks, manoeuvred itself backwards out of the Mini. Melissa followed, and soon they were safely through and into the house.

It was only when the mongrel lay passively on the examination bench that she had second thoughts about asking for the man's help, since he was standing beside her now, hands thrust deeply into the pockets of his joggers, looking at her with a sharp interest. He could, after all, be anybody.

'You're here to see Mr Tremaine?' she asked, trying to share her attention equally between dog and man.

'I am indeed.'

Melissa nodded and resisted the urge to ask him what his business was. Sunday was her day off and she was only here in an unofficial capacity, but it was puzzling to find a total stranger in the house and the place deserted. 'Is there something bothering you?' he asked, catching her stare.

'No, not really.' For reasons she didn't care to think about it was important to her to show him she was neither flustered nor uncomfortable in his presence but in control of the situation. 'Since you're here,' she said stiffly, 'you might as well hold him while I wash my hands.'

'Sure thing. A road accident, I suppose?' Reaching out, he held the dog firmly but in a gentle manner and was rewarded with a ferocious bout of finger-licking.

'I'm afraid so … and it was my fault. He just appeared out of the blue. I suppose I ought to count myself lucky that it was a Sunday – the roads were quiet and no other motorist was involved.' Melissa adjusted the blinds in the room so that she could check the dog's eyes in darkness. Returning to the bench, she shone her light into them, checking for reflexes. Happily, the pupils constricted immediately.

'And you're not hurt?' he persisted.

'No. A bit shaken, I suppose. There was one very kind man who took the trouble to help me.'

He began to hold the dog more firmly as the wet nose sniffed the air with renewed zest when light was returned to the room. 'Your patient seems to be recovering quickly, by the feel of the struggle he's putting up,' he remarked.

Melissa decided her newly found helper was predictably beginning to tire, and in a few moments, thoroughly fed up, he would make some excuse to be on his way.

'Do you think you can hold him a little longer, make sure he doesn't back off the table?' she said. 'I want to check his gums.'

'Fire away!'

This was not the reply Melissa had anticipated, and, somewhat puzzled by his reaction, she began an inspection of the dog's mouth. Satisfied with the healthy gums and set of white teeth, she turned her attention to the side wound. 'This needs cleaning … do you think you could carry on holding him tightly?'

'I'll certainly have a crack at it.'

'I hope you have a fairly strong stomach,' added Melissa, thinking she would give him fair warning. The last thing she wanted was a swooning male. If he was aware of the repercussions of internal injuries, for instance … but then he wasn't a vet and couldn't be expected to know the dangers. The stranger simply smiled at her and offered a charming grin as a reply.

'That was a lucky guess of yours, as it happens,' she said as she began cleaning the wound. 'It isn't too deep and it won't need a great deal of stitching.'

'Good. As you say, a lucky guess.' But then to Melissa's complete astonishment he added, 'You'd better get cracking with the patching up before this little bundle gets overly frisky and decides he doesn't like the look of me.'

Melissa's large grey eyes widened in surprise. With her mop of dusty blonde hair curling untidily about her face and her freckles dotted in abundance across her nose she looked, as her grandfather always told her she looked, a mere slip of a girl. That she had reached her twenty-second birthday always gave rise to much discussion between them, her grandfather invariably having to count backwards to the very year she was born to convince himself.

'It's not up to me to diagnose...' Melissa enlightened him, feeling distinctly unnerved by his manner. 'Only the vet can dispense treatment, and as he isn't here at the moment—'

'You're a fully qualified veterinary nurse, aren't you?' the man interrupted.

'Yes, but that's not the point.'

'Do you mean to say you're just going to leave the poor creature like this until someone shows up?'

'I don't think it's any of your business,' she answered crossly. 'Mr Tremaine won't be far away. He'll be here soon.'

'But can you take that risk? How long are you going to delay, when if as you say all that's needed is a few small stitches?'

A perfect stranger talking like this to her! 'Of all the nerve!' she gasped, her temper rising. 'This is a medical matter and nothing at all to do with you!'

'Now you're being foolish! If you can treat him, go ahead. Who else is there to see? The animal isn't going to thank you for prolonging his misery. Just get on with what you have to do.'

Melissa was so lost for words, she barely noticed that she was being handed the local anaesthetic from the trolley. Taking it, she forced her concentration back to her patient, vaguely aware that she was about to perform the suturing whether she liked it or not. She proceeded to squirt the anaesthetic into the wound and then waited for it to take effect. Rather than engage in further conversation, she made another inspection of the furry body, telling herself that now she had started the job she had better complete it with as much brevity as possible.

'You're a brave little chap,' she whispered into the perked ear. 'Now I'm not going to hurt you. Lie still for a moment and we'll soon have you as good as new.' Threading the suturing needle, she underwent a nasty prick of conscience. She shouldn't really be doing this without her employer's authority, but somehow...

'Is there something wrong?'

'Certainly not!' She wasn't going to let a total stranger dictate to her, and, dropping some of the measured antibiotic powder neatly into the wound, she added authoritatively, 'Hold him still, please!'

The dog behaved himself well and allowed her to carry out the suturing without any difficulty. After she had cut the third and last thread and given an intramuscular injection Melissa wondered if she should apply a dressing as an external protection.

'Hardly necessary to add gauze … if that's what you're thinking. At the rate he seems to be recovering,' and the dog instantly sprang into life as if he knew what was being said about him, 'he'd only rip it off himself and probably cause more damage.'

Melissa nodded. 'Yes, I'd decided on that, but how did you know what I was thinking?'

'You've done a great job with the suturing. Firm and well placed…'

'Thank you, but–'

'What would you like me to do with him now?'

Melissa forgot about the telepathy, returning her gaze to the dog, who was panting healthily and looking as if he didn't have a care in the world. 'I think he must be a stray,' she said. 'I'll phone the police later and ask them if a dog answering his description has been reported missing, but I don't suppose they'll be able to help. By the looks of his tangled coat and the lack of flesh on him I should think he's been wandering for a long time. Meanwhile–'

'A nice warm recovery cage and a little milk?'

Melissa nodded again. 'Now why did I have the feeling you were going to suggest that?'

'It's your animal ESP,' he commented drily, and followed her with the dog in his arms to the recovery-room. 'He's a lovely fellow, isn't he? What name shall we give him for the time being?'

'We?' Melissa froze. She stared incredulously at the man with the shock of dark brown hair and beguiling smile who was settling the animal into a cosy bed. 'Did I hear you say *we?*'

'You did indeed.' He got up and strolled over to her, and quite suddenly everything about him struck her at once – the deep-set eyes so brilliant in their depth of colour, the firm mouth smiling at her now transforming the features she might very well have described as 'chiselled' into smoother, leaner contours. While in a vague sense he seemed familiar she was quite certain she had never seen him before – a face like this she would have remembered. Darkly tanned skin with thick brown hair – he would not be the type lost easily to memory.

'I think introductions are overdue – although I did try to say who I was,' he added apologetically. 'I'm Gareth Tremaine, Gordon's long-lost son.'

Melissa's heart plummeted. She ought to

have guessed who he was; all the clues were right before her eyes and ears if only she had been observant enough to pick them up. Standing before her was the one man she had been dreading meeting. She had known he was coming … the return of Gordon Tremaine's son to help dissolve the practice. But his arrival was planned for next week, certainly not today.

'Well, I don't know what Dad's been saying about me,' he laughed thinly, 'but by the look on your face I don't think it's entirely to my benefit!'

'I … I'm sorry, but it's a bit of a shock. Your father wasn't expecting you just yet, was he?' she said.

'Guess he wasn't. But I plan to get the business side of things concluded as soon as possible. I managed a flight out of Sydney sooner than I thought and took a couple of days in Los Angeles on my way across.'

She made an effort to smile and held out her hand. 'I'm Melissa Moon – but you probably know that already.' He took hold of her hand and shook it warmly, but she withdrew her fingers quickly. In a sense she was shaking hands with the last of her hopes to establish a career, a career that had enabled her to live with her grandfather at Sandy Lane.

While she listened politely to his conversation she found herself remaining aloof, remembering that it was this man who was forcing Gordon into selling out. As a vet himself Gareth could have quite easily persuaded his father to sell to another vet, but instead the Tremaines had given in to the tempting proposition offered by a large development company. No doubt Gareth had pocketed a substantial sum for his own purposes ... why else would he turn up after all these years?

'You let me treat the dog,' Melissa interrupted, her animosity rekindled. 'You should have been the one to treat him, not me.'

Gareth Tremaine raised a dark eyebrow. 'Oh, come on, it was nothing much... I did try to introduce myself, if you remember? Besides, I had the feeling you'd make an excellent job of things yourself, and I was right, wasn't I?'

Melissa felt the colour rush to her cheeks. 'What if I'd made a mistake or there were internal injuries? The dog still isn't out of danger yet.'

'But you didn't make a mistake. And I don't believe he has internal injuries. If I thought there was any possibility of haemorrhaging I'd have said so.'

Melissa began her habitual count to ten. It almost always worked when she felt her temper under serious threat. But it was not an easy task this time, for he had allowed –

no, *encouraged* her to shoulder an important responsibility which should not have been hers at all. No wonder Gordon Tremaine had been so upset about his son's relinquishing all interest in the practice! Knowing that Gareth had such excellent qualifications and yet had decided to fritter them away drifting around the world from one country to another must have been a bitter disappointment for him.

'But I had no authority to treat the dog ... don't you see? It's against all the rules!' Melissa persevered in spite of finishing her count.

'You haven't broken a single rule. I gave you authority, remember? I told you to get on with the job and you merely carried out my instructions. What harm was there in that?'

'But it's not the way it should be done.'

'Look...' Gareth scratched his head in bewilderment '...don't let's get off to a bad start. Let's change the subject, since we can't agree. I'd really appreciate your telling me something about the running of the practice. There are points I have to be sure of.'

She looked at the man with the greeny-flecked eyes and the unruffled manner and relented just a little bit. He was making an obvious effort to put her at her ease, and the thought struck her that she ought to be cordial, if only for Gordon's sake – but it wasn't going to be easy. She had taken an instant dislike to Gareth Tremaine, and above all she did not trust him. 'Your father could tell you all you want to know,' she said stiffly. 'I'm sure you won't need me to tell you anything about the running of the business.'

'Dad has taken Mother out for a drive and then to a meal, at my suggestion. He left me Walter Forbes' telephone number ... he's your locum, I understand? But we don't seem inundated with casualties, and I'd like to familiarise myself with the books. Can you stay for a while ... that is, if you feel up to it?'

The reaction of knocking over the dog had left her feeling drained, although in spite of her annoyance at Gareth's irresponsible attitude, knowing she had contributed towards the recovery of the dog had made her feel better. If she hadn't been forced into treating the animal she would not have enjoyed the enormous gratification she felt now – even if it wasn't rightly hers to have.

'My grandfather thought I was only going to buy some newspapers,' she explained. 'He'll be wondering what's happened to me...'

'Ah, yes, I'm sorry, I almost forgot. Dad told me you lived with your grandfather. Would it be possible to telephone him? I promise not to keep you beyond a cup of tea in the kitchen – and perhaps half an hour in the office?'

Reluctantly Melissa telephoned her grandfather, hoping he might ask her to return straight away. As it was, an old friend of his had called and they were absorbed in a game of chess. She made her way to the kitchen at the rear of the big house with a feeling of gloom. During her four years with the Tremaines she had come to think of the place as a second home. Leaving work was going to be as traumatic as leaving Grampa, and yet here she was, putting herself out to be helpful to the one man who was the cause of all her problems. But she consoled herself with the thought that she was helping the Tremaines and resolved she would do her best for them.

In the kitchen Gareth had already made himself at home, brewing a pot of tea and setting out on a plate some of Mrs Carter's famous fruit cake. Melissa sat down at the table and, despite her initial reticence, they soon began to discuss the running of the practice and some of the more unusual clients. As she knew nearly everyone by heart she found she was taking great satisfaction in being able to introduce them to Gareth. He seemed genuinely interested, asking many pertinent questions, and temporarily she forgot that his purpose in returning to England was the breaking-up of his father's business.

'I didn't think a one-man practice would be so organised, Melissa,' he told her. 'You seem to have all the information at your fingertips.'

She laughed, her grey eyes lighting up with pride. 'Some people think because we're only a small–scale practice we don't have modern methods, but when I joined your father four years ago he was already computerised. Your parents had plans to expand on a large scale...' Melissa sighed, remembering the initial excitement of her first few months. But then, quite out of the blue and for reasons which were never disclosed to her, the ideas had been slowly dropped. 'Your mother's a wizard at reception, apart from being a skilled nurse, and they've worked so hard to build this practice...'

Gareth nodded. 'You're sorry to see it fold up?'

'Of course I am!' Melissa answered, shocked at his question. 'And I think your parents must be mortified.' Then she remembered her manners and tried not to let her true feelings show. 'But it's none of my business, Mr Tremaine. None at all.'

He drew her empty cup towards him and refilled it with steaming tea. 'The name is Gareth. You don't mind if I call you Melissa, do you?'

'You already have,' she answered tritely. Now that their conversation had diverted from the running of the practice she wasn't prepared to extend any personal intimacies. 'Is there anything else you want to know?' she asked in a businesslike tone, and when he didn't reply, apparently lost in his own thoughts, she said in a firmer voice, 'I suppose you'll be re-settling our clients with other vets? Most of them have depended on your father for a good few years.'

Gareth seemed to sense the change in her attitude and sat back in his chair, studying her. She was uncomfortably aware of her old jeans and baggy jumper and wished she'd bothered to tidy herself up. Not that it mattered, it wasn't as if she was out to impress him – that was the last thing on her mind!

'Why do I get the impression,' he said, narrowing the glittering green eyes to slits, 'that you've taken a dislike to me? I'm sorry to be so direct, but I'd appreciate you being frank in return.'

Melissa tried not to look startled, because she sensed a reaction was exactly what he wanted. He boasted little diplomacy, probably aiming to shock and so disadvantage her. But if it was a truthful answer he wanted, she was more than happy to provide it.

'I've nothing against you personally,' she answered, savouring the sense of relief she felt at being able to speak her mind, 'but if you really want to know my opinion I'll tell you. I think this is a good practice with plenty of potential. Your parents haven't treated their clients purely as business investments – which is a rare quality these days. I think they would have liked their work to go on ... if there were someone they could rely on to take it over.' She held his gaze and with great satisfaction gave him one of her no-holds-barred smiles. 'You did ask,' she concluded.

The telephone rang in the hall, and before she could get up from her chair he left to answer it, leaving her with the richly satisfying feeling that he was carefully digesting her remarks to the full, and whatever his reply, it would make little difference to her personally, for her job was coming to an end anyway.

When he returned, by which time Melissa had cleared the cups and washed them up and was ready for whatever verbal onslaught he might have hatched, Gareth merely stretched his long body, peered lazily out of the window, then turned to her and beamed a charming smile. The man has a skin as tough as a rhinoceros, she thought, and averted her eyes.

'Could you show me where we keep the records?' he asked, sounding as though he hadn't heard a word she had said. 'Somebody called Stopes is complaining about a foal not responding to treatment. Dad apparently went out there last week. Does the name ring a bell?'

Melissa had no need to look at the records, for she recalled the difficult case, remembering the endless problems it had posed for Gareth's father. The man ran a smallholding which necessitated veterinary treatment, but he was so mean he'd often bludgeoned Gordon Tremaine into doing work for hardly any fee at all.

'This is a good example of how much patience your father has,' explained Melissa proudly. 'He obliges this man simply because if he didn't, the poor animals would never receive any proper treatment.'

Gareth nodded, but said nothing as Melissa walked back through the house with him to the large front office where the records were kept on computer. She inserted a disk into the machine, waited for the screen to display the details, and soon all the information was there before their eyes.

Gareth bent over her, reading the details. 'Injections to help the mare ... prescribed treatment both for the mother and her off-spring ... and not a penny from Mr Stopes?'

'Heavens, no!' exclaimed Melissa. 'Your father's long given up the battle. Mr Stopes is very slow to adopt any ideas that might cost time or money. I went out there once to deliver a prescription for your father and I could see at a glance that his place is terribly dilapidated. The fencing, for instance, is in a dreadful state.'

'He'll have to change his ways,' commented Gareth with fervour, 'if he wants to survive any more winters. Dad notes that the foal he saw doesn't look as if it's thriving. I suppose we're expected to dash out and get Stopes out of the mess he's in.'

Melissa's heart lurched. If Gordon had been here he would have visited the smallholding irrespective of whether or not he got paid. But his son was a different proposition. She could see quite clearly that he was adopting a tougher attitude.

'Would you be prepared, now we're in the office, to go through a few more of the difficult cases with me?'

She stared at him, unable to believe his lack of interest in the plight of the foal. 'Aren't you going to visit Mr Stopes?' she queried. 'What about the foal?' Was Gareth Tremaine heartless enough to allow a defenceless animal to suffer just because the man could not or would not produce the fee? Even if the business was being dissolved and he had no responsibility to his father, surely he had a moral duty to perform?

He seemed not to hear her question, saying, 'If it's your time you're worried about, Melissa, I shall see you're reimbursed.'

'I'm afraid I can't stay any longer,' said Melissa, beginning to seethe.

'Now what's wrong?' he asked with a sardonic scowl.

'I do have a life of my own outside the surgery, and I seem to have spent the best part of the day here … but that's nothing compared to the welfare of an animal.' Her words spilled out now as though they simply had to be voiced. 'Certainly I could show you another half a dozen examples like Alfred Stopes, but I wonder what you have in mind? Are you intending to collect debts personally just to make sure you're not deprived of a penny?'

She gulped, tilted up her chin and headed for the door. Outside in the fresh air she took a deep breath, then climbed into her Mini and crunched into first gear, but it was only when she was halfway home, her temper just beginning to cool, that she remembered why she had been at the surgery in the first place. Her patient in the recovery-room! She had been too interested in squabbling with Gareth to observe one of the most important rules. 'The welfare of the patient is of the utmost importance, Melissa, never forget that,' her employer was perpetually reminding her. And what had she just done? She'd left the poor animal without checking his condition and without leaving any details for Gordon, allowing her temper to get the better of her.

Gareth Tremaine had managed to shed yet

another responsibility on his first day home. He had driven her to say and do all the wrong things and would probably be wallowing in a gloat of self-satisfaction, thinking he could dismiss her without a moment's prick of conscience. The burden of guilt, of neglect, had fallen squarely on her shoulders. She had been too busy with Gareth's limitations to notice her own!

CHAPTER TWO

Grampa Moon munched at his toast. 'There's something up, my girl – and no use denying it,' he said at last, studying her from under a thick hedge of eyebrow. 'I can read you like a book!'

Melissa cupped her dainty chin in her hands and rested her elbows on the table with a big sigh, a bowl of cornflakes untouched in front of her. 'It's my job... I wouldn't be surprised if I didn't have one today!'

'But I thought Mr Tremaine was going to keep you on for another couple of months?'

'He was...' she said.

'Then what's happened to change that?'

'I suppose it was the way I spoke my mind yesterday. In retrospect it was tantamount to

34

resigning … but Gareth Tremaine is simply impossible! He even goaded me into breaking one of Gordon's most important rules.'

Her grandfather got up from the breakfast table and put a comforting arm about her neat shoulders. 'You were upset! You'd had a nasty accident, it's only natural you should let off a bit of steam. And I can guarantee you this – if he provoked you that much, you'll have worried him double. Nothing like a bit of straight talking to clear the air. And rules, Melissa, are sometimes there to be broken.'

Her full lips curved upwards, into an immediate smile. 'I'll tell that to Gordon when I see him this morning,' she laughed lightly. 'But I really do think I've put my foot in it this time.'

'And it's such a pretty little foot,' came the chuckled reply. Observing her with his usual perspicacity, Grampa sank into his chair by the hearth. 'Your Gareth Tremaine might not be as bad as he seems. Don't make up your mind until you've something to go on. You're a touch … impetuous at times, just as your father was.' Melissa remembered the fair-headed, blue-eyed man who used to swing her up on his shoulders when she was very small. She had her mother's freckles and translucent skin, but it was her father's impetuosity that she was so regularly reminded she had inherited!

'I'll have to go to work now, Gramps, or at least to what's left of it,' she informed him breezily. 'Have you everything you need for the day? What have I forgotten?'

He stamped his foot irritably. 'Women! Always fussing. As if I haven't got enough to put up with!' Then a broad smile stretched over the wizened face and Melissa got a wink for her trouble.

The day was bright and crispy fresh as Melissa drove to work. She imagined lots of things as she drove, none of them very pleasant, the rehearsal of her explanations sounding less watertight by the minute. As she parked the Mini and clambered out it was Gordon Tremaine's voice which echoed across the car park, and Susie, his four-year-old boxer bitch, who came galloping into Melissa's arms.

'Hi, Susie!' Melissa fondly petted her and stroked the velvety tummy as the dog rolled over.

Gordon grinned as she approached his young assistant. 'Now if I rolled over on the ground do you suppose I'd get as much attention?'

Gordon was a handsome man despite his collection of sixty years, with thick grey hair and broad smile. He was so like Gareth she wondered how she could possibly have missed the resemblance. She returned his smile, relieved that he had retained his usual sense of humour, an indication that perhaps he might not be too upset with her.

'Sorry we missed you yesterday, Melissa ... but I hear you and Gareth got to know each other well enough without formal introductions. Come along into the house and have a cup of tea before we start.'

She could tell nothing from Gordon's tone of voice, and she wondered just how much his son had told him. Tempted to divulge the facts herself, she was about to begin the saga just as Gordon's Land Rover chugged into the car park.

'Gareth's back,' Gordon observed brightly. 'He went out to Stopes place last night and again early this morning to give the foal treatment. It'll be interesting to see how he got on with our Alfred.'

Melissa blinked back her surprise, watching Gareth walk over to them looking, as far as she could see, a different person from the man she had argued with yesterday. He wore a sober tweed jacket, well cut grey trousers and a white shirt complemented by an unremarkable dark blue tie. His hair was slicked back into place and he carried Gordon's spare case.

'Hello, Melissa,' he called amiably. 'And how's our clever little nursing assistant this morning? Ready for another emergency op?'

Melissa's surprise flared to annoyance. There it was, directly he spoke – the mocking tone. 'Sarcasm,' her grandfather had always told her, 'is the lowest form of wit,' and she wished earnestly that someone would remind Gareth Tremaine of this.

Gordon, however, dispelled her irritation by uttering a new revelation. 'The suturing you performed on our patient looks perfect this morning and as clean as a whistle.'

'I … I'm relieved to hear it,' gulped Melissa. 'You weren't annoyed that I went ahead–'

'Certainly not. It was an emergency, you made a decision and stuck to it. Besides, you had Gareth to back you up.'

Melissa opened her mouth and promptly shut it again as Gordon dashed off to answer the telephone ringing in the house.

'Credit where credit is due,' Gareth told her, then added, as though relishing every word, 'and you'll be pleased to know I carefully checked your patient and entered all the relevant details on computer after you decided to vanish yesterday.'

Melissa had prepared herself for this, knowing he would not let her off lightly even if he had not divulged the whole story to his father. But if he thought he could use this as a form of blackmail...

'I understand you've seen Mr Stopes?' she asked without hesitation, completely ignoring his statement.

Gareth's eyes twinkled merrily and she realised she had only made herself look more foolish.

'I did indeed ... and a funny sort of a fellow he is too!'

Melissa waited for more details, received none, and decided her best course of action was to follow Gordon as quickly as possible into the house, where a third party would no doubt prevent another catastrophe. But a large hand stretched out and caught her arm. 'Could we try to get along with one another today, Melissa – if only for Dad's sake?'

He was right, of course. Gordon should be the last person to suffer from their personal clashes. At least Gareth had enough sense to realise that. Perhaps all Gareth really needed was a simple reminder about an old-fashioned English tradition called etiquette. But for now, she would adhere to Grampa's warning, curb her impetuosity and allow him the benefit of the doubt. 'A very sensible suggestion,' she answered magnanimously. 'It was a bad day yesterday for both of us. I was upset about injuring the dog and you were probably exhausted from your long journey.'

'That's better,' he said, interrupting her as seemed to be his custom. 'Now you've come down off that high horse of yours we're going to get along very well.'

Melissa blanched and with difficulty held on to her smile, thinking as long as he didn't labour the point of the high horse things would be all right.

'I was wondering … why don't we have dinner together then perhaps … later … we can get to know each other on a more friendly basis?'

The smile faded from Melissa's lips. So it was blackmail after all! In return for keeping her job, she would have 'to get to know the boss's son on a more friendly basis'.

'I could say I was washing my hair,' she answered slowly, aiming for maximum impact, 'or I could say I was already going out, but I don't intend to lie. The truth is I'm prepared to work with you on a professional level until you sack me – and quite honestly I couldn't care less when you decide to do that. I hope I make myself quite plain?'

Almost before she had stopped speaking, Gareth's handsome face crinkled up and he broke into a gust of hearty laughter. 'Perfectly plain,' he gasped, and for several long, intensely humiliating seconds Melissa was subjected to his continuing mirth. 'You can't blame a guy for trying,' he managed at last. 'But I suppose a girl with your sort of looks is used to a more subtle approach.'

She heard the sound of her breath catching in her throat and she simply could not produce an answer. The trouble was, his effrontery made her so cross she could think of nothing as rude to equal it! Fortuitously, a call from Rose standing at the French windows of the house gave her time to regain her composure. Both Gareth and Melissa waved their acknowledgement, knowing it was time for surgery to begin. Still with traces of laughter on his face, he said as they began walking together, 'Cheer up! Most girls would take being asked out to dinner as a compliment. Frankly, I can't see what you're getting so het up about.'

'No, I don't suppose you can,' muttered Melissa, keeping her attention focused on the house and striding onwards. 'But I'm *not* most girls. I'm me. And I think you have a darned cheek in supposing I'd even consider going out with you! You're not back in this country two minutes and you think everyone should simply bend over backwards to do as you want!'

She turned abruptly on her heel and marched into the house, realising as she went that it was the second time in twenty-four hours that she had allowed him the satisfaction of goading her – and what was worse, he seemed to be enjoying it.

Gordon Tremaine stared at his son in disbelief. 'But how on earth did you manage to persuade old Alfred to mend his fencing, Gareth? He flatly refused when I spoke to

41

him about it, even though I warned him that his mare wasn't getting enough fresh pasture to sustain her milk flow.'

It was just before surgery, and Gordon had settled himself on the corner of the office desk while Melissa tapped away at the computer keys, entering new details of the Stopes case.

'I did happen to mention the problems we had in Australia with our grazing land,' Gareth replied with a grin. 'If we didn't fence properly we'd have intruders making themselves at home in no time, thinking they'd come across the land of milk and honey.'

Gordon clapped his hands in delight. 'And I'll bet Alfred couldn't wait to get to his fencing! You touched a sore point there – we've had a lot of trouble in the locality.'

Gareth seemed to be enjoying himself, knowing Melissa was being subjected to his amusing rendition of the Stopes case. 'What I did bring to his notice,' he went on, undaunted by her flagrant uninterest, 'was the current vets' fees charged abroad. Unless people are covered by insurance the charges are exorbitant. Alfred Stopes went a rather peculiar blue colour when I itemised a few. And when I said he was going to have to find himself another vet he nearly had a fit! I was of course referring to your retirement, but he must have supposed I was talking about his debt. Consequently he produced payment like a rabbit from a hat.'

'What details shall I enter?' asked Melissa coldly, her eyes glued to the screen of the computer. If she had to put up with Gareth's company she was determined to listen with an air of sustained detachment.

'I've persuaded Stopes to feed his mare oats and flaked maize,' Gareth answered her pleasantly. 'They're high in protein and good for milk production, which is the whole crux of the problem. I've suggested lucerne, comfrey and roots and any green succulent foods.'

Melissa nodded, computing as he spoke. 'That,' continued Gareth, 'plus the meadow hay and a good field, should do the trick for the foal's continuous supply of milk. I've also worked out a supplementary diet. Stopes moaned like blazes at first, but this morning I think he's come to terms with it.'

'You've achieved the impossible, Gareth,' remarked his father. 'All these years and I've never found a way of handling him properly.'

'Just luck, combined with a few colourful stories from the bush. If you don't look after your stock properly you might as well give up before you start. I think he got the picture. With a little more coaxing I reckon I'll have Alfred Stopes keeping his livestock up to scratch and paying his bills too.'

'Good news,' agreed Gordon. 'But

unfortunately it's too late for us now to reap much of the benefit. I mean, with my retirement and the business sold off...'

Melissa glanced up, sensitive to her employer's regretful tone. It surprised her to see that Gareth was hesitant in making a reply. Whether or not it was because of her presence there she couldn't tell, but what she was not blind to was the look which passed between father and son.

After a busy morning, Gordon and Melissa went to inspect the frisky-looking animal wagging his tail in the recovery-room. 'Gareth's named him Flash,' the vet told her. 'Appropriate, don't you think?'

Melissa bent over Flash and stroked the soft hair which had obviously been given attention, and with a feeling of guilt she remembered it was not she who had given it. 'The wound isn't looking too bad at all,' she said to cheer herself.

'You did very well, Melissa, I'm proud of you. Gareth explained that you lost no time in dealing with the problem, even though I'm sure you must have been pretty upset yourself.' Gordon patted her shoulder. 'It's a bit like learning to ride a bicycle really. If you fall off the idea is to get on and have another go. I'm sure you managed to put the accident behind you, knowing you'd helped the dog afterwards.'

'I was worried I didn't have your authority,' she explained.

'Extenuating circumstances!' Gordon grinned mischievously at her. 'How about taking him for a walk this afternoon across the fields if we're quiet? He looks up to it, don't you think?'

'No internal injuries?' she asked.

'No reason to think so. But what I am worried about is his immediate future. Gareth wasn't able to get any clues as to ownership from the police yesterday.'

So Gareth had remembered to phone the police too. Trying to dismiss the irritation she still felt at her own negligence, Melissa forced herself to concentrate on returning to her work and helping Gordon with a final patient.

'This is William, but we call him Billy for short,' said a young woman, handing over a delightful spaniel puppy. Hanging on to her mother's skirts and eyeing the vet with mute suspicion was a little girl of about seven or eight.

'Don't let him do it, Mummy!' she shrieked suddenly. 'He'll hurt Billy – I know he will!'

Gordon stroked the puppy and then knelt by the whimpering child. 'I promise you Billy will be all right. He'll grow up to be happy and healthy once he's had his injections, just like you.'

'That's what's worrying her,' said the mother sharply. 'Trudi had an injection for tetanus recently, and it upset her so much. She begged me not to bring Billy here today.'

Gordon took hold of the child's hand. 'You do want him to be strong and healthy, don't you? Not sick or poorly?'

The blonde head peeped out of the folds of her mother's coat.

'This injection inoculates Billy against nasty illnesses we call distemper and parvo, hepatitis and leptospirosis. Not very nice names, are they? And not very nice to catch either. So the people who love animals have made a very special medicine, to protect all dogs like Billy from a very young age. Just like Mummy got you protected the other day.'

Trudi's gaze was now fixed on Gordon's face. He raised one hand to stroke Billy, whom Melissa was holding tightly, and used the other hand to gently squeeze Trudi's plump fingers reassuringly. 'But if you want to take Billy away, and risk it...? Well, what do you think, Trudi?'

The little girl blinked inky blue eyes and looked up at her mother. Then she turned to gaze at her puppy and bravely nodded her head. 'I don't want Billy to get ill,' she decided.

'Then we'll give him this very special

46

medicine, shall we?'

Trudi nodded again, and presently a little smile touched her lips.

Gordon deftly filled the syringe while Melissa stroked Billy, taking up his attention with a few kind words, and soon the needle was in and out without a flinch from Billy.

'He didn't cry like me!' said Trudi, delighted.

'That's because animals have a special magic,' whispered Gordon in her ear. 'The magic love that makes you and your puppy understand one another. He trusts you to do your best for him since he can't talk in a human language. They're very sensible beings, often more sensible than us.'

Afterwards, explaining to Trudi and her mother about booster injections and proper certification, Melissa began to wish Gareth had been on the scene. His father possessed such an aptitude for helping both animals and people alike. It was such a pity that Gordon was being forced into retirement while he was still so active.

Lunchtime arrived, and Melissa accompanied Gordon to the kitchen, where Rose and Mrs Carter had prepared a veritable feast. Gareth, right on cue, strode nonchalantly in after being conspicuous by his absence all morning.

'How did you get on at the property developers?' his father enquired, solving the

47

mystery of his disappearance.

Gareth ambled over to the large kitchen table spread with salads and fresh baked bread. 'Satisfactorily. But don't let's talk business during lunch. And what a lunch! Mrs Carter, you're a gem!'

The daily help, proudly displaying her newly permed grey hair and a smart pinafore obviously worn in celebration of Gareth's return home, laid a tray of delicacies on the table. 'T'wasn't all my handiwork, lad. Your mother cooked the soufflé as a special treat, so make sure you have a good helping. Make a change from all that barbecue stuff you've been living off for goodness knows how long!'

Rose Tremaine placed the deliciously puffed soufflé in the middle of the table. Her fresh complexion and dark hair drawn up into a smart chignon bore the faintest dusting of flour, and with jade-green eyes that were exactly her son's she smiled at Melissa. 'Do sit down, dear, next to Gareth.'

Melissa felt her cheeks flush hotly. She perched on the edge of her chair and Gareth raised a teasing eyebrow, but she pretended she hadn't seen and sipped her fresh fruit juice. It was apparent to Melissa that Gareth had returned from the business with the property developers without any ethical qualms at all. It seemed he didn't consider his own parents' feelings, much less hers.

Probably the reason she was still hanging on to her job was that he enjoyed the goading he subjected her to, deriving a secret delight from it. But somehow she managed to get through the meal, and it was by no means too soon for her when Gordon said they must be on their way for afternoon surgery.

Exercising Flash in the fields behind the house, she took deep breaths of sweet, clear air and felt the light breeze blow away the cobwebs. However, her tranquillity did not last long, for when she returned from the walk she was alarmed to hear a hue and cry coming from the car park. Taking a peep over the gate, she saw a rather battered van, more rust than metal, and being roughly pulled from its interior was a large black and tan dog, hackles running the length of its back. Sensing trouble, Melissa quickly went by way of the rear gardens, deposited Flash in the safety of the recovery-room and then sought out the vet in his surgery.

'A Rottweiler,' observed Gordon, peering out of the window. 'And a very large dog at that. It looks as if the young man can't handle him properly.'

'I'll deal with this, if you've no objection, Dad,' said a voice from the doorway. Gareth stood in a white coat, hair brushed back neatly, his tanned face the picture of health. 'Why don't you help Mother with the books this afternoon? I've just left her struggling in

the office. Melissa and I can hold the fort.'
And, not giving her a chance to answer, he
added, 'If there's anything we can't handle
we'll give you a shout, won't we, Melissa?'

Gordon Tremaine, as big as he was, looked
like a little boy who had just been told he
had a day off from school. Finding his voice
after the initial shock of Gareth's businesslike appearance, he answered, 'I'll certainly
not argue over an afternoon's redundancy.
Switch the phone through, Melissa, and
Rose and I will take the calls. Are you sure
you can manage?'

'Perfectly,' Gareth assured him. 'Only I
think you'd better make yourself scarce. I've
a feeling our next client is going to prove
time-consuming!'

When Gordon Tremaine left the room
Gareth glanced at Melissa. 'You don't mind
assisting me, do you?' He said this, rendering
her speechless once again, as if the ill-feeling
between them had never existed, almost as
though they were meeting for the first time.
'A dark horse,' would be Grampa's verdict,
no doubt.

'No, I don't object to assisting you,'
answered Melissa, thinking she had better
say something and not just stand there like
an idiot. 'If it's what your father wants...'

'I'll try to make working alongside me as
painless as possible,' countered Gareth with
a grin. 'Had we better see to our client, do

you think?'

Melissa pulled herself up to her full five feet five inches, thrust back her head and escaped into the hall. She had no time at all to mull over what had just taken place, for the huge dog struggled in, tugging its master through the glass doors. Coal-black eyes glared up at her from behind an ill-fitting muzzle.

'Tell him to heel–' Melissa began to say, but was knocked against the wall as the animal charged past her. More by luck than good judgement the dog and its owner plunged into the empty waiting-room, where Melissa, when she got her breath back, was able to contain them as best she could.

'I can't control him,' grumbled the young man, struggling ineffectively with a piece of rope he used as a lead. 'He's already attacked one dog. And as for people–!'

Melissa managed to get a brief outline of the dog's history and the owner's name and address. She had the growing feeling that this was going to be an awkward case for Gareth. The young man was adamant that he did not want the responsibility of the animal, and it was patently clear that the dog was not going to be easy to handle whatever the outcome of the interview. A few minutes later she relayed the meagre details she had gathered to Gareth in the treatment-room.

'Mr Roper swopped some audio equipment for the dog about three months ago, intending to use him as a guard for his van – he's a mobile disc jockey. But the dog refuses to be kept in the van. Mr Roper says he's destroyed a number of valuable items already. Now it seems he's turned to attacking other dogs, and he's afraid it will be a human next.'

Gareth stood quietly listening. Melissa was appalled at the story herself, knowing that in most cases the unfortunate animal would have to suffer the consequences of human cruelty.

Soon Mr Roper was noisily on his way into the treatment-room with his dog. Gareth closed the door behind them and the Rottweiler, with hackles raised, made low guttural sounds as it sniffed around the room.

'He looks a healthy specimen, Mr Roper. Not too many problems, I hope?' asked the vet optimistically.

The young man shouted abuse at the dog in order to quieten him. The dog went on growling and pulling on the rope. 'There, can't you see? He's just plain mad! I got him because I thought he'd save me money, but this is ridiculous. I've had to replace all the equipment he's destroyed and I've just had to pay out for the dog he nearly throttled. You vets cost a fortune!'

'Was he on a lead?' Gareth asked calmly.

'You mean when he attacked the other dog? You gotta be joking! Time's money, and I don't have time to walk the thing like a lapdog. He got out one day ... broke his way out of the shed I've been keeping him in. Stupid animal!'

'Why did you take him on in the first place?'

'I told you, or at least your girl here. I wanted him as a guard. That's not against the law, is it?'

'No, it isn't. But I think a burglar alarm would have been cheaper.'

'Look,' growled the young man, 'I didn't come here for lectures, so don't go giving me any!'

Melissa watched, heart in mouth, as Gareth's jaw muscle began to work slowly up and down, the only indication of his feelings towards the unsavoury character. Respectfully the vet asked, 'Then what did you come here for, Mr Roper? I'm afraid I can only give you advice.'

The young man looked astonished. 'Advice? I don't want advice. I want the dog put down – and right now!'

Melissa felt herself grow cold. She had feared this was going to be the man's outrageous demand. One of the most distressing parts of her job as an animal nurse was to see any animal in pain, but this dog was healthy and still very young. Looking at

Gareth, she wondered what his feelings were. Was he prepared to extinguish without question the life of a beautiful animal at the whim of a disgruntled human being?

In a voice which was carefully controlled, Gareth said, 'You realise you're asking for a death sentence on an animal which probably hasn't been given a chance? With proper behavioural therapy and possible castration, a dog of this age could be helped.'

'Don't talk to me about help! I've forked out enough already on your so-called help. I fancy I'm doing it a favour paying for it to be got rid of. My mate who had it before was just going to dump it out on a rubbish tip somewhere.'

'But that's just the point. The animal has been passed from one person to another. No wonder it's aggressive! Wouldn't you be if all you ever saw was the pitch-black interior of a van or shed?'

Although Gareth kept his voice steady, the reaction of the young man was to clap his hand on the bench with such force it made Melissa jump, and the dog which had half settled suddenly leapt into an aggressive stance. 'Get rid of it now,' shouted the dog's owner, 'or I'll take it somewhere and do the job myself!'

Melissa dug her fingernails into her palms to keep her tongue in check, and it came as quite a shock when Gareth said in a very even voice, 'Melissa, I believe I can hear the telephone. Would you answer it for me, please?'

'Can you? Oh, yes ... I'm sorry. Will you be able–?'

'I'll be fine,' he said gently. 'Take your time. Don't rush to come back.'

There was, of course, no telephone call. Gordon had switched the extension through to the office or probably the private rooms of the house where he and his wife would be working. Was Gareth about to do as the owner asked? He had obviously decided he didn't know her well enough to count on her full support. Melissa was in two minds herself ... how would she have coped in assisting Gareth? She felt outraged at the ignorance of the man who had taken on such a responsibility and now wanted to dispose of it through no one else's fault but his own.

Just as Melissa had decided she should have spoken up – at least said something on the dog's behalf – Mr Roper, red-faced and with an ugly, supercilious grin on his lips, sped past her through to the glass doors. 'You're all in it for the money!' he shouted sourly before he left. 'Good riddance, if you ask me!'

Melissa stood quite still. A feeling of total inadequacy overwhelmed her. She had become an animal nurse in order to help

save lives, to dedicate herself to the creatures who had no voice to plead with and no
ultimate say in the dispensing of human
justice in the animal world. Her work was
meaningless if she hadn't had the courage of
her convictions.

She walked slowly towards the treatment-
room.

'Come in quietly, Melissa.' Gareth's voice
was low. 'Don't make any move to come
towards me, just do something over there,
like busying yourself with the instrument
trolley, will you?'

Melissa did as she was told. She hardly
dared look across the room as she picked up
the things which needed sterilising.

'Good dog,' murmured Gareth softly
behind her. 'There's a good dog. Sit now.
Sit!' Melissa's heart leapt as she listened to
the repeated commands, albeit interspersed
with a few nerve-shattering growls. She
couldn't resist a peep, and she saw to her
delight the big dog sitting peacefully beside
Gareth. 'If there's no one waiting to be seen
will you fetch a large bowl of milk, please,
Melissa? I'm going to give him a drink after
I've removed this apology for a muzzle.'

Melissa quickly went to collect the milk,
hardly able to believe her eyes and ears.

'Just wait there at the door and I'll come
and get the milk from you,' directed Gareth

on her return. 'Stay, Beetle, stay!'

'Is that his name?' asked Melissa as she handed over the bowl.

'It is, I'm afraid. Perhaps it won't be too late, when we get to know him a little better, to change it.' Then, studying her more closely, he asked, 'Are you worried about aggressive dogs? Would you prefer to go out to Reception?'

She smiled appreciatively, and a sudden warmth in Gareth's eyes induced her to talk to him. 'No, I'm not afraid. I've always loved dogs of any shape or size, and when my parents were alive we kept several of our own. It's only been in later years when Gramps has been a bit unsteady on his feet that we've reverted to budgies or goldfish.'

Gareth returned her smile so warmly Melissa felt a curl in her stomach. 'Beetle does look as if he's responding already,' she mumbled, trying to dismiss the pheno-menon.

'The poor dog's totally confused. It's going to take quite a while to straighten him out.'

'You're going to keep him?' she asked, watching Gareth carefully remove the ill-fitting muzzle. His capable fingers moved deftly around the bristling whiskers with no hesitation at all. This time, Melissa's tummy made a major drum roll as she watched his gentle grace.

Free to drink, Beetle ravenously siphoned down the milk set before him. 'To be quite honest with you, I don't know what I'm going to do with him.' Cautiously Gareth introduced a head-collar attached to a strong lead. Then with the dog at his left leg he opened the French windows leading out to the rear gardens. Rewarding Beetle with a broken piece of biscuit from his pocket, he walked out into the fresh air, beckoning Melissa to follow.

Heel! and Sit! were the two distinct commands she heard given, and after repeated tours around the garden, he led Beetle into the large compound which was sometimes used as summer kennels. Melissa watched, astounded at the immediate response of the dog to kindness.

'He must sense that you're not going to ill-treat him,' she said, watching Gareth fill a bucket of fresh water from the garden tap and place it in Beetle's new home. The dog, who seemed to have an enormous thirst, drank greedily. 'Perhaps he knows you saved his life.'

When Gareth had closed the kennel gate securely, he turned to smile at her. She could see a change in him. It was no more than a subtle shading, something richer, perhaps an animation in the eyes which seemed to light up the whole face. 'You didn't think I'd agree to his demands, did you?' he asked.

Melissa blushed. 'I didn't know what to think. I thought perhaps you'd do as he wanted.'

'You don't know me very well, Melissa.'

'You may have felt you had no choice?'

Gareth shook his head and the slicked-back hair fell across his forehead quite naturally as somehow she knew it would. 'There's *always* a choice. To fight or submit, to love or to hate … to live or to die. In Beetle's case I had a hunch that money would be the optimum.'

'Do you think you'll be able to train him?' she asked.

'I'm going to try. He's only a juvenile and he needs to understand his position in the pack, as it were. He has to be rewarded for good behaviour, introduced slowly to other dogs, and he has to learn what we all have to learn: to transmute his anger.'

'I must admit,' said Melissa candidly, 'I felt swamped with anger at that man's cruelty.'

Gareth nodded. 'A perfectly natural reaction. But don't you think we must learn to change the nature of our anger into a more constructive emotion or we'd constantly be at war with everyone, wouldn't we?'

He was close to her now, the late afternoon sunshine spreading its nimble fingers through the trees and capturing her face in a halo of misty spring light. 'Has any-one told you, Melissa, your freckles glisten

59

in the sunshine?' he asked softly.

She laughed, knowing it was true. And all at once she realised it was the first time she had given way to laughter in his company. The resultant feeling was wonderful. Her body felt light and tingling, and just for a moment she imagined, foolish as it was, she had no desire to keep him at arm's length. There was another side to him, a side which fascinated and drew her in spite of her better judgement. Thinking only of this, she made no effort to move away as he came towards her slowly, hearing the guttural whisper she barely discerned as her own name.

'Melissa...'

For a moment her world stopped still. She experienced for the first time in her life the shock and exquisite pleasure of a body aligning with hers in perfect symmetry as Gareth pulled her towards him. The surprising relaxation of her muscles as he drew her onwards caused no protest to come from her unresisting body, but instead pleasure overwhelmed her, softened and moulded her.

She gave herself up to his kiss, to the shattering insistency of his lips upon hers, and as he demanded more of her mouth, his tongue dancing at the edge of her teeth, she was tempted with all her heart to respond. Involuntarily her arms slid up to his shoulders, not as a rebuff but as sheer delight, feeling the tough curve of his arms, the force beneath the taut cloth of his jacket drawing her relentlessly towards him. With her eyes closed she surrendered, gasping inwardly at her first journey to heaven in the arms of...

And then the gasp was real! In a stranger's arms ... she heard a small voice warn ... and with an effort that made her painfully conscious of her complete lack of strength and his overwhelming power she forced herself apart from him.

His lips seemed to burn and her heart palpitate beyond reason as she opened her eyes and stared breathlessly upwards, seeing a smile of victory turning the corners of his mouth.

'Now that, I would imagine,' Gareth drawled lazily, fully releasing her, 'is another perfect example of a constructive emotion!'

CHAPTER THREE

Melissa sat shaking like a leaf in the Tremaines' downstairs cloakroom. 'How could I ... how could I let him?' she kept repeating softly to herself, patting her flushed cheeks with the palms of her hands.

'Easily!' said another little voice, one which piped up from somewhere in the depths of her being. 'And don't try denying that you enjoyed it ... you'll only be fooling yourself!'

'Oh, shut up!' Melissa answered her other self furiously. 'Who's asking you, anyway?'

She allowed the burning sensation which had been pulsating through her body since Gareth had kissed her to subside before resuming her two-way conversation. Standing up, which wasn't very easy because her legs were the last part of her anatomy to recover, she stumbled towards the hand basin, turned on the cold tap and bent to splash water on her face.

'That's better,' she breathed, dabbing at her face with a soft paper towel. And trying to convince herself she really did feel better, she peered into the mirror hoping to find confirmation of the fact. Instead she found a stranger with eyes glistening lustrously who looked as though she was suffering from shell-shock.

'I can't have ... can I?' she mumbled. And trying to rationalise the way her body had responded, the way she had been tempted to slide her arms around Gareth's strong neck and the desire she had experienced to prolong the moment when his lips had so deliciously covered hers – trying to rationalise these things did no good at all. She couldn't. None of it made sense. And everything had always made sense in Melissa's life. She was a far-sighted person and objective ... she had to be, looking after Gramps! There had never been time for affairs, they just weren't practical. Friendships, yes, but she had always veered away when a relationship became too intense, feeling her loyalties lay with Gramps and his dependence upon her. And yet now, out of the blue, she had let a man she thoroughly disliked, whom she hardly knew, take her in his arms and kiss her ... in no ordinary way either!

'But I didn't have time to stop him,' she persuaded the reflection.

'Liar!' the inner voice echoed. 'You can slap a man's face any time you like, you can struggle, you can kick shins!'

Tiny glistening dots appeared in the corners of her eyes. 'Stop it!' she ordered hotly. 'Stop being so silly! It was only a kiss – it's not the end of the world.' But it felt like the end. How on earth was she ever going to face him, and in front of the clients too? One distressing thought tumbled after another, and when the knock came on the door she almost jumped out of her skin.

'Melissa? Are you in there? It's Gareth!'

Even the sound of his voice sent her heart leaping to her throat. In a croaky voice she forced herself to respond, 'I'm coming!'

A silence of a few minutes preceded a firmer command. 'Melissa, it's urgent. Please hurry!'

She stood, wishing the earth would open up and take her. But there was no escape, she'd have to face him. And more than that, she would have to hide her confusion if she wanted to preserve a vestige of pride. An actress she had never been, but she might as well start learning now ... camouflaging this crazy state a single kiss had landed her in... Gareth didn't have X-ray vision, did he? He couldn't see into her real thoughts!

'Here goes...' muttered Melissa, almost delirious now with indecision, and with her heart racing ten to the dozen, she opened the door – to find the hall empty.

Savouring the few seconds of quiet to compose herself more fully, she walked slowly along the corridor, running her hands over her slim hips, pressing down the green uniform to her curves. At least outwardly she could look presentable, even if she was shaking like a jelly inside.

She discovered Gareth in his treatment-room, bending over a small dog swamped between the folds of a blanket.

'Do something ... please!' pleaded its lady owner. 'I know I shouldn't have left it so long, but each time she strained I thought she'd give birth...'

Gareth looked up at Melissa's arrival. His eyes disconcertingly bored deeply into her own grey, hesitant ones. Melissa looked away – only to hear his voice demanding her attention. 'If you've finished doing whatever it was you were doing, do you think I could have some help here?'

Gareth unwrapped the blanket carefully, then handed the dog to her, an action which necessitated their fingers briefly touching. Melissa found she was unable to stop herself from going pink to the roots of her hair. Luckily the dog's owner distracted them both. 'Tamsin is Mr Tremaine's patient. Where is he? Surely I've a right to see my own vet?'

Gareth smiled politely. 'You most certainly have, Mrs Stroud, and if he were on duty he'd be happy to help you. I'm Gareth, Gordon's son–'

'I don't want a junior, I want my own vet!'

Gareth's face paled and Melissa, for once, was thankful for a difficult client to absorb his whole attention.

Laying the griffon on the examination bench, Gareth began to examine the swollen body, his fingers travelling expertly over the taut skin. 'How long would you say she's been straining?' he asked calmly.

Mrs Stroud shrugged. 'Oh, I don't know, about an hour or so, maybe longer.'

Gareth frowned and shook his head. 'Once a bitch is in labour, unproductive straining and restlessness suggests she needs medical attention. A puppy could be stuck in the vagina, or they may need to be removed by Caesarean operation.'

'Caesarean!' shrieked the woman. 'You're not going to cut her about? You can't … it's unthinkable! I won't let you do it! Your father's never touched Tammy with a knife – never!'

'As you wish,' replied Gareth, straightening his back. 'But I would have imagined that a sensible person like yourself would do everything in her power to save both her pet and help the puppies which so obviously need assistance in being delivered.'

Mrs Stroud froze. 'Oh, God, what shall I do? What shall I do? Don't you understand? Tammy is a griffon bruxellois!'

Gareth agreed that she was indeed a true example of the toy breed, but it made little difference to the fact that her puppies had to be born. Melissa watched the resolute male face smile as though he hadn't a care in the world – and after the incident in the garden too! He certainly was a cool customer! Here she was a mass of nerves, while he was calmly engaging in a verbal battle without turning a hair.

'But will I ever be able to show her again?' persisted Mrs Stroud. 'What if she's permanently disfigured?'

Gareth laughed lightly, showing those delicious white teeth again, and Melissa was not beyond viewing Mrs Stroud's reaction to the smile. She found herself wondering just how many other women had fallen for its charm.

'Whatever gave you that idea?' drawled Gareth. 'Surely the saving of Tamsin's life is your priority? Come along now ... if you were ill and offered life at the price of a tiny scar, would you accept?'

'Yes ... yes, I suppose so.' Suddenly Mrs Stroud burst into a flood of tears, and Melissa found herself, surprisingly, in the role of comforter.

'Mr Tremaine will look after Tamsin for you,' she said gently. 'But you must let him operate or it might be too late. Listen, I'll take you over to Mrs Carter for a cup of tea in the kitchen.'

She glanced at Gareth. 'Thank you,' he mouthed as she led her charge from the room. When Melissa returned, Gareth was preparing for surgery. 'Look ... about what happened in the garden, I'm sorry if I upset you, but there's no need to freeze me out,' he said, staring at her as she began to scrub up beside him.

'Talking of constructive emotions,' said Melissa with as much dignity as she could muster, 'I think all ways round it will be better if we concentrate our energies on our work, don't you?'

'You think so?'

'I certainly do think so,' she retorted hotly, her grey eyes narrowed in anger. In spite of her unresisting body, her mind was still functioning well enough to put this Aussie Lothario in his place!

'If that's the way you feel...' He left his gaze a fraction too long on her to make her feel easy, before shaking talc on to his firm brown fingers and stretching on surgical gloves. 'Tamsin has nothing blocking her passageway, so it's going to have to be a Caesar,' he said, as though a word – or a kiss – had never passed between them. 'Can I leave you to cope with the anaesthetic?'

Melissa nodded and began to prepare the equipment, silently congratulating herself on her first effort at acting the part. She only hoped it would serve as her first and her last for keeping that powerful chest and those eager arms at bay. No matter what she said to him, her heart was still clattering around behind her ribs like the percussion section of a symphony orchestra!

'She's quite frail,' he said, breaking into her reverie. 'We'll give her a short-acting anaesthetic ... watch her carefully ... and hope she's strong enough.' He positioned the griffon carefully in front of him, and when she lay unconscious on her back Melissa handed him the scalpel, snatching back her fingers so that Gareth didn't observe the slight tremble in them.

The incision was swift and sure. Deftly he removed a miniature corpse which Melissa realised had never had a chance of survival. Seconds later Gareth delivered a live puppy, blind and wrinkled but beautifully formed.

'At least he looks healthy enough,' he said, examining Tamsin's son. 'I'm going to close up now. How are we doing?'

'Pulse and respiration fine,' Melissa told him calmly.

'Just the antibiotic, the heart stimulant injection and suturing ... then we're almost done.'

Anticipating his movements as she had been taught to do by Gordon, Melissa worked efficiently beside him, blocking out, as far as possible, all intrusive thoughts.

'I seem to have found myself a girl who doesn't get flustered,' Gareth remarked abstractedly as she handed him the suturing needle. 'It makes a great deal of difference to an operation, you know.'

Melissa blushed deeply. If only he knew what she had been feeling like just before the op! 'Your father's been a wonderful teacher,' she volunteered as she cleaned Tamsin while he dealt with the puppy. 'I managed to gain my Advanced Diploma under his tutoring ... which I don't think I would have done with anyone else. He's been very patient with me. Academically I think I've only just managed to scrape through.'

'Oh, come on!' Gareth exclaimed disbelievingly. 'Where's the confident girl who put me through my paces on an injured animal?'

Melissa's grey eyes twinkled at the memory. 'We're all split personalities to some extent – so psychology tells us.'

He gave a faint smile. 'Let's get our patients into a recovery cage, then you can tell me more. I'm all ears!'

Melissa helped with Tamsin and her son, thinking there were many things she could tell him ... if he were to be trusted! Intimacies both professional and personal. For instance, she could explain that she had always been sensitive to animal needs, so much so that from a small girl she had made up her mind to become a vet. When she had been lucky enough to gain a place at the grammar school she'd made up her mind that nothing would stop her from achieving her ambition. And then had come her parents' accident. Not that she could blame that for her change of mind. Something had simply altered inside her. Grampa said she had grown up quickly, taking on the motherly role too soon ... but with Grampa being widowed, her desire to become a vet had been replaced by the growing need to keep what was left of the family together. The compromise had come when she decided to become an animal nurse. And together she and her grandfather had made a comfortable life together at Sandy Lane.

But surely Gareth Tremaine couldn't care

less about her private life? He was here to meet business ends, any dalliance along the way was probably a diversion from the boredom he was experiencing being home. And it didn't take a genius to know that what had happened in the garden was only a dalliance!

'There's nothing to tell,' she answered as she pulled off her surgical gloves, keeping her eyes averted. 'I mean, nothing that would interest you.'

Gareth turned to her with a wry grin spreading across his face. 'You know your trouble, Melissa? You set standards too high for yourself. You don't relax enough.'

Melissa fixed him with a suspicious grey stare. 'And now I suppose you're going to tell me the best way to relax is to go out for dinner with you this evening?'

He laughed, green eyes sparkling appreciatively. 'I think I deserved that. But yes, it wouldn't be a bad idea.'

'You don't give up, do you? You–'

Melissa watched helplessly as he walked towards her with an intimidating swagger. 'All right, all right! I'm sorry if my sense of humour upsets you. Trouble is I'd forgotten how British people always take things so seriously. I'm afraid living abroad has done me no good whatsoever. I'll try to be a little less disruptive ... to your sense of proprieties.'

She was half inclined to believe him, despite the irony in his voice. But no matter how he tried to present himself and however humane the man was with animals, it was still Gareth who was the cause of the practice closing. It would be foolhardy to allow sentiment to get in the way. She was attracted to him physically, yes, that had been embarrassingly evident. The pull of his physical being was immense even now. She could feel it overwhelmingly as she stood close to him, her mind still boggling over the possibilities of what would have happened if she hadn't broken away from him in the garden. But she had already indulged her over-active imagination too much – nothing could come of irrational daydreaming!

It was at this point that Rose appeared, poking her head round the door. 'Summit conference on the griffon, no doubt?' she remarked.

'Er – yes, yes. Come in,' Gareth told her, pulling back his broad shoulders and stepping away from Melissa. 'All's well, Mother's doing fine having produced one strapping offspring.'

'Marvellous!' congratulated Rose, eyeing them both with faint curiosity. 'Melissa, do you want to be the one to break the news to Mrs Stroud? She's still in a bit of a state; even Mrs Carter wasn't able to comfort her. She seems to have taken a liking to "the nice young lady in green".'

Melisssa eagerly accepted the opportunity to leave the room. Outside in the hall she breathed a sigh of relief. The atmosphere with Gareth had been thick enough to cut with a knife, their vibrations had fairly zipped around the room!

Mrs Stroud, on hearing the news, burst into yet another flood of tears, this time joyful ones, while Mrs Carter sagely observed, 'I knew all along that everything would be hunky-dory. Young Gareth's treading in his father's footsteps, that's for sure!'

When Melissa was able to get away she realised it was already past her time to leave, but Mrs Carter's knack of highlighting a sensitive subject niggled away at her as she took Flash for his last walk through the field. With the property developers about to raze the practice to the ground it would be a fine thing if there were any footsteps left to follow in!

Managing to slip away without bumping into anyone, Melissa drove home, resolving to keep Gareth in perspective. He might be the saviour of all animals, a veritable St Francis of Assisi, but he was still the cause of her having to uproot her career, a career which she had always imagined to be stable. But try as she might to think objectively her mind stubbornly returned to the moment when he had drawn her into his arms and

73

kissed her. There had been nothing in the touch of Gareth's lips that she had not enjoyed, wanted more of ... and the worst of it was, the expression in those eyes stubbornly blotted out all her other thoughts.

Eventually Melissa realised she must have been sitting in her Mini for light-years before she realised that Grampa was staring out of the window waiting for her to come in.

The smell of slightly damp wood crackling in the hearth pervaded the cottage. Melissa remembered as a child making figures out of the scarlet flames, and yet all she could see now was the flickering face of Gareth Tremaine.

'Was I right?' muttered Grampa from his chair at the side of the hearth. 'That young man ... he didn't turn out to be so bad, after all?'

Melissa lay languorously in front of the fire, her hair still wet from a stringent wash, a wash which hadn't succeeded in washing Gareth from her thoughts. Her pale face, overshadowed by the grey lustre of her large round eyes, grew rosier in the reflected warmth. 'I really don't know, Gramps. I thought I was a judge of character, but this time...'

'You do mean this vet of yours, I suppose?'

Melissa giggled, her eyes creasing as they

always did when she really laughed. 'Not my vet, Gramps, not even the practice vet. Actually I'm not sure what he is. Gareth Tremaine is a puzzle, a man of paradoxes.'

'And what's that supposed to mean?'

Melissa sighed thoughtfully, her curling hair fluffing out from the heat of the fire like strands of Christmas tree silver. 'Well, for a start, I thought he was determined to retrieve the bad debts of the practice before the development company moved in ... at a cost to our patients' welfare. I suppose I judged him as mercenary.'

'And?'

'And ... he retrieved the money without any trouble at all, but he also made sure the animals were treated properly.'

'And that surprised you?'

'Yes, in all honesty it did,' she admitted.

'What other conclusions have you arrived at?'

Melissa smiled to herself at the memory. 'Today he saved a young dog from being put down... I really thought he might not have the backbone to argue with the man, but I was wrong. He's even adopted the dog. Some would say it's a silly thing to do. As you know, Gramps, we'd all be overloaded with animals if we did that every time a hard-luck story came into the surgery.'

'He sounds like a very nice young man. Very nice indeed.'

'That's just it,' sighed Melissa, 'he could very well be putting on an act for everyone's benefit. My first impression of him was that he was egotistical, arrogant, smug–'

'You liked him, then?' asked Gramps.

Melissa burst into laughter. Her teeth sparkled in the firelight and her skin shone fresh as a baby's. 'Let's just say half of me likes him and then the other half doesn't trust him. Anyway, I don't suppose it matters very much. It looks as if the development company project is going ahead.' Her laughter died as she thought of the prospect. 'And soon I'll be out of a job.'

Grampa Moon looked around for his favourite tobacco, stuffed his pipe with practised ease and then avoided adding a match, a habit which he had maintained ever since rejecting the weed. 'Don't be too sure, lass,' he said softly.

When Melissa arrived at the surgery the following morning, Rose Tremaine was giving Susie her early morning run and waved excitedly as Melissa parked her car beside the Land Rover. Susie bounded over, and at the back of the house Melissa could hear the throaty bark of Beetle announcing that he was doing an excellent job of guarding.

'I have some wonderful news!' Rose whispered as she linked her arm through Melissa's. 'Will you be surprised when I tell you Gareth has asked us to put a hold on our plans to sell?'

Melissa's grey eyes widened as Rose went on to ask, 'Is it you we have to thank for Gareth's change of mind?'

'No, of course not!' Melissa managed to gasp. 'At least, what I mean to say is–'

'What you mean to say is...' interrupted a deep voice, 'quite the opposite of what you do say. Aren't all women the same when it comes to a straightforward answer?' Gareth appeared beside her, coming out of the early morning mist like a ghost.

Seeing him again so suddenly, Melissa was sure the acute embarrassment was obvious on her face. But Rose continued light-heartedly, 'Now the last thing we need is any of your conundrums, Gareth! We don't understand them and we haven't got time to fathom them out. Besides, your father is over there checking his watch. If you really do insist on finding out more about the practice – and the workings of the female mind – you'll have to bear in mind his insistence on good timekeeping.'

'Assuming the two are related?'

'Very much so, Gareth. Don't forget it's said that behind every good man there's an equally–'

'Good woman?'

'Precisely.'

'I've a feeling we're now nearing dangerous territory and the hackneyed subject of my bachelorhood,' grinned Gareth, 'so I think I shall make myself scarce. Come on, Melissa, we've work to do.'

Melissa found herself being forcefully propelled towards the house, only to be intercepted by Gordon rushing down the steps. 'Morning, Melissa. You've heard about our stay of execution, then?'

'Oh, come on, Dad, it's not like that,' said Gareth with a quick glance at Melissa.

'No, not quite,' Gordon laughed lightly. 'The fact is we've been bouncing around a few ideas ... extending the practice rather than giving it up. Large animal work, all that sort of stuff.'

'Do you mean you're not going to sell out to the development company?' asked Melissa, making sure she had heard correctly.

Gordon looked at his son and smiled. 'I think not. We've found a way round one of our biggest problems.'

'That's wonderful news ... but I'm afraid I've applied for that job in London,' Melissa blurted out.

'Is it definite?' Gareth asked abruptly.

She shook her head. 'Not yet. But I do have to let them know soon. I've the relevant qualifications ... and the senior partner of the veterinary hospital has offered me staff accommodation until I can find a flat.'

'It sounds like a very good offer,' Gareth

murmured softly.

'I'm afraid we shall have to continue our discussion later,' interrupted Gordon, realising there were clients waiting. 'Let's get this morning over with and we can talk at lunch. Don't worry, Melissa, we're not going to strong-arm you into anything you don't want. Rose and I know how much you were looking forward to a change of scenery. A talented girl like yourself can't be expected to put up with the confinements of a small-scale practice such as ours. I know at your age it's imperative to broaden your horizons.'

'It won't be small-scale for very much longer, not if I have anything to do with it,' interjected Gareth.

'But I don't–' began Melissa, then gave up as she realised she was alone in the office. Reeling from the impact of the shock, she found it hard to believe there was still a chance that she might be able to stay in Dorlington. Naturally she hadn't wanted either Rose or Gordon to know just how much she relied on her job, nor how disappointed she would be to give it up. That wouldn't have been fair. But at this late stage for such a turn of events … it must have something to do with the potential of the business and Gareth's discerning eye. For instance, a financially secure future without having to lift a finger to secure it!

Ten minutes later, with her doubts freshly resurrected, Melissa found herself trying to placate an irascible ginger tom Gareth was trying to examine. The nervous scrutiny of a perplexed owner made this procedure even more difficult.

'Bert never misbehaves,' complained the thin-faced man. 'I'm at work all day and I live by myself, so Bert's often left alone, but in the three years I've had him none of the neighbours has complained. Not until now, when a new family moved in next door. They're dog people, you see. Every time Bert goes into their garden they unleash their monsters on him and then complain that he's upsetting them.'

Gareth eyed Bert with respect. His ears lay back along the crest of his head, whiskers vibrating, green eyes seeking the first possible opportunity to claw his way out of the situation. Mr Trimble edged away from the table. 'He's a nervous wreck, poor thing. It's those ridiculous dogs with spots all over them. I'm perfectly sure they molested him yesterday.'

'Dalmatians are usually friendly creatures...' Gareth persuaded Bert back into a crouching position and ran his hand gently along the line of the feline back to the tail. Immediately Bert reared up with a frightening hiss, claws at the ready.

'Look, it's obvious, isn't it? He's frightened out of his wits!' complained Mr Trimble.

Melissa watched Gareth stroke Bert and very cautiously examine the area around the cat's tail. If his attitude towards her when she had first met him had been less infuriating and more like the careful consideration he was displaying to a feline on four legs, her own back might not have gone up in retaliation. What was it about the man that caused her to be on the defensive all the time? And why should she have the feeling there was more to Gordon's news than met the eye? Somehow the details just didn't seem to add up.

'It's not the Dalmatians who are at fault,' Gareth was saying. 'Cats usually hold the monopoly over dogs very well. Bert isn't frightened, Mr Trimble, he's in pain. See for yourself, two small puncture marks just beginning to form an abscess.'

'You mean those tiny marks there are causing all the trouble?'

'They are. Small puncture wounds forming a tense lump – I'd say from a fight with another cat. Left any longer they'd become a fully blown abscess which would have to be drained and might cause Bert a great deal of discomfort. I'm going to clean the wound and give him an antibiotic. Would you mind holding him securely for me?'

Mr Trimble, as white as a sheet and with a

film of perspiration on his top lip, shook his head vigorously. 'I'm not terribly good at this, I'm afraid. I think I'm going to have to sit down somewhere ... I feel a bit funny.'

There seemed hardly any need for Melissa to suggest the waiting-room. Mr Trimble was gone in a flash, leaving Bert staring warily at Gareth. 'Looks as if it's Bert Trimble versus medical science! He's not going to like this one little bit.'

'I'll just get our cat gloves,' suggested Melissa, refraining from remarking that claws were only drawn for a very good reason, a manifestation common also to the female sex. 'Anything else apart from the antibiotic?' she asked instead.

'Just you,' muttered Gareth, raising his eyes from the ginger tom and settling them on her. For the moment she was rooted to the spot. Two little words strung together and added to the dark and dreamy depths of those green eyes were having a ridiculous effect on her.

The provider of distraction was Bert. He decided to make his escape and leapt from the table. At the same time, Melissa roused herself from the trance into which she had fallen and landed simultaneously with Gareth on the furry body just about to disappear under a cupboard. With her hands locked securely around Bert, she felt Gareth's strong fingers close over hers and discovered she was trapped.

Bert, in his wisdom and understanding, took full advantage of the situation, wriggled himself free and bolted for another hidey-hole.

'Tell me,' drawled Gareth, refusing to let go of her hands, 'why are you making such a big deal over staying on at the practice? The money's good enough, isn't it – or are you trying us out for a fatter wage packet, is that what you want?'

This time, jumping to her feet and snatching away her hands, she hissed her disdain at Gareth. 'You really are the limit! Just because you've got a mind that revolves twenty-four hours a day around money you suspect everybody else of being exactly the same!'

'Money is what makes the world go round … or so they say,' he answered scornfully, rising from his haunches to lean by the door. 'And what's so wrong in wanting a pay rise anyway? It's a perfectly understandable gambit on your part.'

'You make it sound as if I've been planning all this!' exclaimed Melissa, her cheeks burning with humiliation and anger. 'Well, just let me tell you, Gareth Tremaine, I couldn't care less what you suspect me of, and I don't want your ridiculous job either!'

Gareth raised a dark eyebrow, his cool stare emphasising a painful silence and making her suddenly realise just what she had said.

'In that case,' he conceded contemptuously, showing the edge of white teeth between constrained lips, 'here's Dad now. I think you'd better tell him what you've just told me. Then with a bit of luck we'll all know where we stand.'

CHAPTER FOUR

Gordon sped in with a belated knock. He stood uncertainly, beginning to mutter. 'Er – sorry... I didn't mean to disturb you, but you've got visitors, Gareth. I'll take over here if you like.'

Gareth nodded, eyeing Melissa speculatively. For a tense moment she believed he would reap the satisfaction of her unwise retaliation by informing Gordon of her hasty decision. Of course she had sounded like a petulant child! But hadn't he driven her to say what she had? If he decided to make a show-down of it now, Melissa saw there was no way out other than to stick to what she had said. Lifting her chin, she returned his stare defiantly.

'Who is it, Dad, did they give names?' Gareth asked brusquely, still with angry eyes fixed on her.

'Friends of yours from Sydney – better go and see for yourself,' Gordon told his son. 'Everyone's in the kitchen. And, Gareth...?'

'Yes?'

'Don't forget to leave yourself free at lunchtime. I really do want to explore plans for our future in more depth – and we won't be able to do it with guests in the house.'

Slowly Gareth's demeanour began to soften, his glance shifting impassively from Melissa. 'I'll pack them off to the Queen's Head in Dorlington,' she heard him say as he moved into the hall. 'There's nothing an Australian likes better than a British pub.'

Melissa expelled a deep sigh of relief as Gareth disappeared, feeling her taut facial muscles relax under the friendly gaze of her boss. Left alone with Gordon, their attention fell upon Bert, who was in the middle of a grooming session on the bench.

'Now let's have a look at this old fellow,' he coaxed, picking up Bert with an experienced hand and re-examining him. 'Hmm. Puncture wounds ... they don't drain easily. Can be quite nasty at times. We'll clean him up and give him some antibiotic. Keep his claws covered with the gloves, will you, Melissa?'

It was just as they were finishing the treatment that Gordon remarked casually, 'Rose and I are going to miss you like the very devil, Melissa. That is, if you do go...'

'Sweet of you to say it, Gordon,' Melissa answered, feeling ashamed of herself for having thrown in the towel to Gareth so easily. 'But your news has come as rather a shock today. Just give me a little time, will you?'

'All the time in the world,' Gordon agreed, handing her a quieter Bert.

When Bert was safely in his cat box and on his way home, Melissa returned to clean the treatment-room. Lost in her work, she found her thoughts turned to Gareth and the way she had reacted to him in the garden. Even the memory of his physical proximity sent an army of shivers along her spine. The way he had touched her, caressed her, seemed to blind every avenue of sensible thought. She had to fix the words in her mind, 'Are you trying us out for a fatter wage packet?' to stir up her anger for him. And even then the recipe didn't seem to last very long.

Just as she was preparing to drive into Dorlington for a snack lunch, Gordon met her in the hall, his face unusually flushed. 'Fancy a bite to eat, Melissa? Rose says only if it's convenient and you haven't anything planned.'

'Are you sure?' Melissa asked in surprise.

'Our guests didn't react very well to the suggestion of the Queen's Head. And don't ask me why, I haven't a clue what's going on!'

Melissa refrained from observing that he wasn't the only one, and reluctantly she followed him through the old house to the kitchen. At least with two more males at the lunch table the sore subject of her staying on at the practice would almost certainly not be brought up.

'Lunch in the dining-room,' grumbled Mrs Carter with a look Melissa recognised as rank disapproval. 'I'm sure I can't see any reason to have to lay on a banquet just because of visitors!'

Gordon vanished ahead as Melissa countered tactfully, 'I expect Mrs Tremaine enjoys having her son's friends home every once in a while.'

'Not this one she won't. Not after all the tears this morning.'

Melissa stared with uncomprehending eyes. 'Tears? Did you say tears?'

'I most certainly did. A bucketful of 'em. She says young Gareth ran out on her. Fairly knocked Mrs T sideways, it did.'

'I don't quite understand...'

Mrs Carter shook her head. 'Dian Taylor's her name. She's a little madam who's chased him all the way from Australia. Had the gall to turn up her nose at my cake and say it was fattening! The brother's not too bad, mind. At least he's not fussy.'

'You mean Gareth's friend is a lady friend?' queried Melissa.

'Supposed to be a model ... thin as a rake, like a blooming skeleton. She's pretty ... I'll agree she's pretty, but I'd eat my hat if she was his type.'

Melissa stood still, wondering at her own stupid naïveté. Why had she assumed Gareth's visitors to be male, and why, above all else, was she feeling like this, so desperately disappointed?

When Rose appeared, Melissa recognised a similar disillusionment registering in the thin smile and agitated expression. 'I think we're ready for lunch now. Melissa, are you coming?'

'You go in and I'll bring the soup,' ordered Mrs Carter airily. 'Thick vegetable. Let's hope this won't be considered fattening!'

Accompanying Rose into the dining-room, Melissa wondered just what lay before her. She was soon to discover. Gordon headed the table, looking glum, while Gareth on the far side sat next to a young woman with a stunning suntan, happily chatting away. Her jet hair was braided fashionably into a long plait, and something about her china-doll expression made it necessary to take a second look just to see if she was real. Beside her sat a young man who immediately caught Melissa's attention with his bright blue eyes. His mop of fair curling hair bore no resemblance to his sister's dark locks, but his smile, like hers, was full and eager.

'Dian and Peter, let me introduce you to Melissa Moon, our very capable nursing assistant,' said Rose, sitting down next to Melissa. 'Dian and Peter are going to be spending a few days with us while they're in England.'

Dian extended a long slim arm across the table. 'Hi, Melissa!'

Melissa smiled and shook Dian's hand – then found her fingers clasped in the iron grip of Peter. 'Pleased ... very pleased to meet you, Melissa,' said Peter, holding on a little too long to her hand for it not to be noticed by one and all. His voice had the deep, rough twang of Australia and it seemed to rebound around the room. Melissa couldn't help glancing at Gareth, who sat with a cool look in his dark eyes, quietly observing her every movement.

'Gareth didn't tell me there were such pretty girls in his home town,' Dian said acidly as they began the first course. 'No wonder he was in such a rush to get back home!'

Gareth smiled, bouncing off the young woman's obvious innuendo. 'Our British girls aren't all hockey-sticks and horses, Dian ... haven't you ever heard of the sweet English rose?'

'I have!' exclaimed Peter, digging in

ferociously to Mrs Carter's lunch. 'And I reckon we've got one sitting at the table.'

Melissa looked up to the assembled faces all turned towards her. If she imagined her acting days were over she was wrong. This was going to be a fight for survival... Dian was giving her looks to kill, Peter was making the matter worse by beaming a fresh smile at her, and Gareth's infuriating grimace told her that some new suspicion was stirring in his mind ... for after all it was Rose and not him who had asked her to join in what was obviously a family affair.

'What do you do in Sydney?' Melissa asked, nervously trying to cover up her predicament.

'I model swimwear,' Dian told her rather coldly. And by the time the sherry trifle came to the table, ladled out by the unusually heavy hand of Mrs Carter, Dian was explaining the peculiarities of the catwalk, at least relieving Melissa of any further need to extricate herself from the conversation.

At coffee, Gordon sat twiddling his thumbs and looking distinctly put out. When he brought himself to interrupt it was with an apologetic smile. 'Dian ... Peter, you'll have to bear with us. We're in the middle of making some rather important plans. Gareth has decided to consider the feasibility of coming into the business as a junior partner.'

'But I thought you were retiring, Mr Tremaine?' Dian asked, undaunted.

Gareth moved uncomfortably beside her. 'That was the original plan, but things have changed quite a bit since I've come home.'

'You mean you had no intention of coming back? You really did walk out on me?' Dian said, looking accusingly at Gareth.

'There was nothing to walk out on,' Gareth replied silkily.

'Hey, come on, Sis, don't let's spoil lunch,' Peter persuaded his sister gently.

Dian cast aside his attempts. 'Oh, it's all right for you, Peter, you didn't come all the way across the world looking for the person you love!'

Peter stared directly at Melissa, his blue eyes twinkling. 'Didn't I?'

'Please...' Rose Tremaine's usually soft voice heightened in her attempt to defuse the argument. 'I'm afraid, Dian, you and Gareth will have to work out your differences in private. We've only another half-hour before we begin the afternoon's clinic. Please try to bear with us just until we decide on this issue.'

'But it does involve me too,' protested the young woman, unwilling to be silenced. 'I do have a successful career of my own to follow. If we come to live in England I'll need time to make arrangements ... although that won't be too difficult as the agency I work for has a branch in London. In fact it would suit me quite well.'

Melissa felt shock waves course through her ... an occurrence she was becoming used to these days. Hardly daring to put a name to the way she was feeling, she wondered if Dian really had come all this way for the love of Gareth.

Gareth stood up, flicking his gaze over Melissa. His eyes were remote and expressionless and she could only look back at him with her own confused and bewildered stare. Then, politely pulling Dian's chair back, he said, 'We'd better talk about this some other time, Dian. Listen ... why don't you take a shower and freshen up and I'll meet you later? Peter, do you want to join us?'

'No, thanks,' Peter answered laughingly. 'I don't think Dian would thank me for playing gooseberry.'

Although Melissa couldn't be sure Gareth's face tightened a shade at Peter's response. Since she was feeling slightly shattered herself at the disclosure that Dian was still Gareth's girlfriend, she had no wish to prolong her own discomfort by witnessing the rest of the conversation.

'If you'll excuse me,' Melissa said quietly to Rose, 'I'd better get back and open up.'

'See you later,' whispered Rose, but just as Melissa made her escape Dian leant across and brushed Gareth's cheek with her pale pink lips, leaving an indiscreet trace of colour. 'I'll slip into something a little more comfortable, darling. See you in an hour or so?' As she left the room she looked back at Rose and said, 'I'm sorry to have got upset this morning... I was so confused – jet lag, I guess. But now I've seen Gareth I feel just fine.'

Melissa had no wish to hear more. She hurried to open the surgery, thinking there could never have been such a fool as her. Dian was one of the most beautiful women she had ever seen, and she was Gareth's. With his looks he must have left dozens of women in his wake. What in heaven's name had prompted her to think the embrace he had lavished on her was anything more than a whim? Life was all fun to Gareth Tremaine, he didn't take anything seriously – he was an opportunist, a man as shiftless as sea and sand! It was ironic that a man like him made a woman feel so vulnerable, so conscious of her sexuality, and, if she was honest with herself, wasn't that how she had been feeling ever since she met him?

As two o'clock struck, Melissa reached the large glass door and turned round the sign to open. Distracting her from her thoughts, an elderly gentleman stepped into the porch and walked slowly through. 'I don't really know if you can help me, miss,' said the man, squinting at her and removing his trilby hat. 'I might even have got the wrong vets, but I think the name was Tremaine. I can't quite remember...'

'And you're my Good Samaritan!' cried Melissa, suddenly recognising him without his hat. 'You were kind enough to help me with Flash on that awful morning.'

The elderly man glowed with pride. 'You've got a good memory, miss, especially as it was such a shock for you. I'm Stanley Tubbs, by the way.' He held out his hand.

'My name's Melissa,' she said warmly, grasping it.

'I just wished there was something else I could have done for you and the dog. You see, my Rex died last year just before Christmas and I know exactly how you felt.' He looked down at the threadbare brim of the trilby. 'You feel so helpless.'

'If it weren't for you,' said Melissa gently, 'I wouldn't have managed at all. There were other people there, but it was only you who were kind enough to help me.'

'Do you need some help, Melissa?' A voice made her swivel round. Gareth stood, hands in pockets, behind her.

Melissa fought to keep her voice steady. She really hadn't expected him back – after all, he had guests to see to. 'This is Mr Tubbs,' she told him. 'He helped me with Flash on Sunday.'

Gareth's pensive expression changed into

one of welcome. 'Come in,' he said, stretching his long arm behind Melissa to push back the door. Just a small touch of his arm on her back felt like a charge of electricity and she had to concentrate all her efforts on recovering her equilibrium.

'Flash, as we've called him, is well on the road to recovery,' Gareth explained. 'Would you like to see him?'

'Are you sure you've got time? I don't want to put you out … it's Mr Tremaine, is it?'

'Tremaine Junior,' said Gareth easily.

'I had a cross collie just like him, you see,' enthused Mr Tubbs as they all walked through to the garden kennels. 'Rex was his name. And he was fifteen.'

Gareth nodded. 'Flash is about four or five. And in spite of the fact that he's so thin, under all that hair he's in relatively good condition. I've just been introducing him to another dog, a Rottweiler we call Beetle who isn't as well mannered.'

In the kennels the dog held out his paw and a wrinkled human hand reached down to take it. 'I knew from the moment I saw him he was a lovely animal. It's that look in his eyes – it goes right to your heart, doesn't it? Someone's bound to claim him soon…'

'I wish that were the case.' Gareth shrugged his large shoulders. 'It looks as though he's going to have to go into kennels as soon as he's fit enough.'

'Oh, but he can't! Surely you can find someone to give him a home?' protested Mr Tubbs.

Melissa shook her head sadly. 'Suitable homes aren't so easy to come by. Societies like the RSPCA and the PDSA have to deal with thousands of dogs like Beetle and Flash each year. Dogs who never have a loving home.'

She thought of her own life and how devoid of security it might have been if not for her grandfather. And yet Gareth, coming from a loving and secure home, had displayed such indifference to parents who had provided him with a secure background.

Gareth bent to ruffle Flash's coat. In spite of everything she found herself overwhelmed with feeling for him, an emotion which seemed to go beyond reason, the mere proximity of his presence causing an undoubted stir of physical attraction deep within her. He was a man who defied sensible or rational thought. She should know better than to be daydreaming like this, for surely it was obvious that Gareth took all his affairs lightly, even to the extent of travelling continents to avoid the commitment of one relationship in particular.

'It's quite expensive these days,' Gareth was saying, oblivious of her scrutiny, 'to take on a dog like this. He'll have to have his vaccinations, at least two to protect him for a full year, and regular boosters to maintain his immunity. He'll also need to be wormed and bathed in a concentrate powder to prevent mange.'

'What about his bad side?' asked Mr Tubbs forlornly.

Gareth smiled and looked at Melissa. 'As far as his wound goes, it's healed remarkably well … thanks to this young lady.' And when he looked at her, Melissa warmed to the lingering look in those expressive eyes … yet did she want him to imagine she was yet another conquest? After all, she had been an easy target in the garden. And what about all the hours afterwards devoted to thoughts of him?

Mr Tubbs was staring at them, his gaze shaking Melissa out of her fantasy. 'I'd have him if I could,' he said wistfully. 'I've missed Rex so much. But you see, I manage on a pension. Vaccinations and powders are well beyond my limit.'

When Mr Tubbs had gone, Gareth cast his eyes over the Rottweiler lying full stretch in the sunshine. 'I'm going to have to postpone Beetle's training this afternoon... Dian's nervous of dogs.'

Beautiful women have a habit of taking priority, thought Melissa scathingly as she turned to walk into the house.

'You're still cross…' Gareth walked beside

her, his dark head inclined to one side. 'Did you mean what you said about quitting?'

Melissa reminded herself that if she decided to stay with the Tremaines she had to make sure from this moment on that her job was top priority. She could not afford to become emotionally involved, yet an alliance between them was of the utmost importance if she was going to work with him to the best of her ability. Had she forgotten how much Gramps had sacrificed for her? Surely controlling her emotions and her roving imagination was not too much to ask in return. 'It was rude of me ... before. I lost my temper – I'm sorry. My grand-father tells me it's a failing of mine.'

'Apology accepted,' said Gareth, his green eyes egging her on. 'So I take it you're staying?'

'I...' began Melissa, wondering herself just exactly what she was going to say, when another voice reverberated across the garden.

'G'day!' Peter strode towards them, his broad shoulders swinging easily and his golden hair highlighted in the soft sunshine. Melissa felt Gareth stiffen beside her – or did she imagine it? 'How do you two feel about coming out on the town with Dian and me?'

Melissa saw that Peter had changed into casual gear, smart trousers and a T-shirt, brave for this time of the year, and perfect for the display of muscle rippling beneath the short-sleeved shirt. She couldn't help looking at the way he moved, not particularly lithe and athletic as Gareth's movements were with his supple, lean body, but more with the stance and durability of a strong, square physique.

'What exactly did you have in mind, and when?' Gareth asked before Melissa had time to answer for herself.

Peter flashed a smile at them. 'I'm taking Dian to London tomorrow ... dropping her off to the modelling agency while I call on some of the petroleum companies in the city. I'm in market research, you see. We'll be back pretty late, might even stop over to see some of the sights ... how about the weekend?'

'OK as far as I'm concerned,' Gareth drawled carelessly. 'As a matter of fact, I wouldn't mind a change of scenery.'

Melissa looked at both men, wondering when they were going to include her in the conversation. Did Peter take it that Gareth's answer was reflective of her feelings? If so, he would have to think again.

'I'm sorry, Peter,' she said in a firm tone, 'but I've made other arrangements for the weekend.'

Peter cast his intense blue gaze upon her and to her surprise merely raised his hand in a fleeting gesture of impatience. 'And miss the chance of a lifetime in being wined and dined by a man who's so lonely for good company he'd go to the ends of the earth to get it, my little English rose?'

Melissa caught Gareth's expression out of the corner of her eye and had the fleeting satisfaction of seeing the green eyes glint in a not too friendly fashion in Peter's direction. Was it this that caused her to join in with the Australian's good-natured banter? Whatever prompted her to suddenly mellow and turn her large grey eyes warmly on Peter, she never did quite fathom out. Laughingly she returned, 'If your idea of wining and dining a girl is as generous as your flattery, Peter, I don't see how I can refuse...'

'That's settled, then!' Peter exclaimed, hanging on to her gaze with a look that did not belie his satisfaction in winning her over.

Gareth was quiet as they walked back to the house for afternoon surgery. But as Peter went to search for his sister, he stood in Melissa's way, making it obvious he was not finished with her.

'I pity the poor fellow you're standing up for some fast-talking Romeo,' he said between gritted teeth. 'Or do you have your men so wrapped around your little finger you don't even have to make up excuses any more?'

Melissa gasped, words failing her. How suddenly Gareth changed! One moment she felt she was on exactly the same wavelength with him, the next he was taking the wind completely out of her sails by accusing her of flagrant deception.

'I ... I don't think it's any of your business who I'm going out with–'

'I thought as much. Quite a little Jekyll and Hyde, aren't we, Melissa ... but then you did give me a clue once, didn't you? What was it you said... "We're all two people" – yes, that was it. Full marks for the practical demonstration! You've illustrated your point perfectly.'

Melissa caught her breath, the tight coil of tension swelling in her stomach. The audacity of the man ... hadn't he tried to make a date with her in much the same way as Peter, except Peter had come right out into the open in such a way that she hardly felt she could refuse him? It was almost as though Gareth was jealous of Peter, and perhaps he was! Maybe coming up against such a virile ego for once in his life he felt threatened by competition. Well, as far as she was concerned he could think what he liked!

'You really will have to excuse me, Gareth,' she said coolly, although she was fuming inside and longed to retaliate. 'I have work to get on with ... work I consider far more important than standing here defending myself against such childish remarks!'

Drawing a deep breath, she squared her slim shoulders and purposefully walked around him. But when she found herself in the safety of an empty office she fell against the door, her heart beating wildly and perspiration beginning to dampen her body. Gareth Tremaine defied description! He had the audacity to accuse her of two-timing when he himself had betrayed Dian!

Melissa shivered at the memory of the betrayal. How she hated her weak and vulnerable body. How she hated her gullible mind, one which was, even now, thirsting after a dream. A dream which would not, after all that had happened, disappear and leave her in peace.

CHAPTER FIVE

'Fiddlesticks!' exclaimed Grampa Moon. 'Sitting around all day making raffia baskets doesn't interest me one little bit.'

Melissa bit her tongue as she accompanied her grandfather into the church hall. 'This is the first and last time I'm ever going to be roped into going to one of these churchy functions!' he threatened.

Ten minutes later Melissa was on her way to work, breathing a sigh of relief. Friday had come in like a lion, with her grandfather refusing to go to the church club, and a bribe of apple pie for dinner had to be resorted to. Oh, well, that was the least of her problems! She mulled over the one very big problem, the one in the shape of a dark-haired, green-eyed human being who had gone out of his way to show his lack of interest in her for the past few days.

Melissa stopped at a set of red traffic-lights and lost herself in their symbolism. Red for danger, a clear enough warning. Even ferocious bulls understood the meaning of that one particular colour. And hadn't there been ample warnings with Dian's arrival? More so since she had stayed in London with Peter, leaving Gareth to his own devices, walking around the house like a zombie. Oh, he'd been polite enough, but the sense of humour Melissa had taken such a dislike to at first seemed to have died, and in its place a distant reserve had sprung up. Was he feeling guilty about the way he had kissed her? Was he afraid she would tell Dian in a moment of pique? Was he regretting his behaviour so bitterly that he was going to inordinate extremes to make it plain he had no interest in her?

'If that's the case,' Melissa mumbled angrily beneath her breath, forcing the gear into first as the light changed to amber, 'he needn't worry. If he thinks I'm the sort of girl who's going to chase after him just like Dian and probably dozens of others, he's got another think coming!' Angrily she glared out of the window, then curved her mouth upwards as she resolved that today would end happily – if it had not begun that way.

Pulling up in the practice car park, Melissa prepared herself to meet Gareth. She was learning fast. But it wasn't her real nature to be cool. She loved life and people and her work, but with Gareth the whole atmosphere of the place had changed. So much so, that she had actually been considering her alternatives, the very worst one ... of moving away and putting the Tremaines behind her.

'Morning, Melissa,' Gordon welcomed her as she walked into the office. 'Glad you're early ... I had a bit of bad news last night. I'd like to talk things over with you.'

Melissa felt her heart sink. Was everything destined to go wrong today? Gordon observed her reaction and mustered up a grin. 'Don't worry, it's nothing serious. I'll just give Rose a shout.'

Presently Rose joined them bearing an armful of warm woolly jumpers. 'Take these for the car, will you, Gordon?' she asked, tipping them into her husband's arms. 'There are the photos to go too ... and our walking boots and anoraks.'

Gordon raised his eyebrows to Melissa and stumbled off under the mountain of clothing. 'I hate to think what we'd have to take if we were going for longer than a week!'

Rose flopped on to an office stool and smiled tiredly at Melissa. 'We've got a family hiccup. My sister Agnes had an accident, not a serious one, but she'll be humping around a plaster cast for the next month or so. Their car lost its brakes, went off the road and ended up in a ditch. Her left leg's fractured quite badly.'

'Oh, dear ... and it's Scotland, isn't it?' Melissa asked uncertainly. 'An island on the west coast somewhere?'

Rose nodded. 'Trust me to have my closest relation living on a remote island! But the plain fact is, when Glasgow General let her go home, she and Robbie are going to need help ... they're farmers, only two homesteads on the whole of the island.'

'So you're going,' said Melissa slowly.

'First thing in the morning, I'm afraid,' Rose nodded. 'The helicopter is booked to fly her from the mainland on Monday.'

'Oh, Rose, I'm so sorry ... as if you haven't enough on your mind! Is there anything at all I can do to help?'

Rose pushed back a curl of dark hair and looked at Melissa with a wry smile. 'As a matter of fact, yes. I've a real favour to ask. But don't feel you have to ... it's just a thought.'

'Anything,' Melissa answered eagerly.

'It's the leaving of the practice we're

worried about. Gareth can cope, of course, and Walter Forbes will come in. But we've got two dogs boarding with us, Susie to look after, and no doubt there'll be emergencies ... that's a guaranteed fact at weekends. Mrs Carter is already in a panic about having guests in the house; I can't ask her to look after the telephone as well...'

'You'd like me to do more hours?' Melissa asked unreservedly.

'More than that. I know it's a presumption, but I wondered if you'd move in ... just for a few days, as you did last year when Gordon had flu. It was such a help.'

Melissa sat very still, ears ringing with a most peculiar sound. It was as though every noise inside and outside of her body was magnified, her pulse racing like a train, as Rose gazed expectantly at her.

'Ah, I wondered where everybody was.' Gareth stood at the office door, not yet clothed in his white coat but wearing casual trousers accentuating the muscular but lithe arch of his thigh muscles and a light sweater clinging to the shoulders that now eased themselves to relax against the door-frame. His hair was freshly wet from a shower and his eyes surveyed the two women with curiosity. 'What's going on, you two? You look like women conspiring ... and from my experience the end result of a female conspiracy isn't usually to a man's benefit!'

Melissa was almost relieved to hear his old sense of sarcasm back again. But in the same moment her relief changed to a mild panic when Rose said, 'I've just been asking Melissa about staying over.'

Gareth's face darkened, though with remarkable control he kept his voice light. 'I thought we'd settled that point last night. It isn't necessary to ask Melissa. We can ring for an agency nurse, they're bound to have someone.'

'They haven't,' said Rose with a sigh. 'I phoned first thing and they've got no one with the qualifications. I wouldn't be asking Melissa if it weren't absolutely vital.'

'Then I'll manage myself. Good grief, there'll be a houseful here – Dian and Peter are coming back at the weekend. If I'm desperate I can always call on them.'

Rose gave a hoarse cry of disbelief. 'That's what I'm trying to avoid! Pleasant as your friends are, Gareth, I can't see Dian getting up in the middle of the night to nurse a sick post-op patient. Why should she? She's a guest here, not an employee. You can't expect people to wear hats that don't fit them... I should have thought you of all people would know that, Gareth.'

Melissa clenched her fingers against her palms. She could see Rose was tired and her patience sorely tested, and it was obvious that Gareth resented the implication that he could not handle the situation independently. What was worse, he was probably thinking the girl he had flirted with so indiscriminately might be coming far too close for comfort to reveal his indiscretions. Something about this idea gave Melissa sudden lift of spirits. Now he would know what a sense of alarm was like and perhaps experience some of the cocktail of doubts and anxieties she herself had been subjected to over the last week. Impetuously she decided she would add a little fuel to the fire. 'Rose, I said I'd do what I could to help … and I'll stick by that. But if Gareth would prefer not to have extra help–'

'Nonsense, Melissa!' Rose stood up, giving her son a long look. Two pairs of identical eyes met. 'Gareth is just being polite,' Rose said firmly. 'It was only yesterday he was telling Gordon how much he admired you! Needless to say Gordon's head hasn't recovered its proper size yet. "Home-grown produce", he so ungallantly calls you, my dear.'

Melissa smiled in spite of the fact that Gareth's lips were forming a thin straight line.

'There's only one small problem,' she mumbled, enjoying having her own back on the man who thought he could get away with any indiscretion he cared to perform. 'And that's Gramps. Not that he minds what I do ... and if I were in London he'd simply have to get used to me being away. But I'm not so keen on him being entirely alone. I'll just check with him first...'

'Of course,' Rose said sympathetically. 'I quite understand.'

Gordon marched into the office, patting fluff from his tweed jacket. 'Rose got you all shipshape, has she?' he asked jauntily.

Gareth shrugged and for the first time looked at Melissa. She knew he had absolutely no option other than that of going along with the plans. After all, if he had returned to England with nothing save a nose that smelt out money, or, as Gramps would say, he was a man who was 'on to a good thing', asserting himself at this point might only serve to alienate his parents.

The emerald eyes, so usually frank in their appraisal of her, regarded her with a softer expression. Melissa felt a rush of dismay at her own impetuous behaviour. Was she merely getting back at him because of Dian? Had the feeling she experienced at the lunch table light-years ago been a form of jealousy? And yet she had mentally accused Gareth of this same emotion as she'd readily agreed to go out with Peter ... enjoying every minute of Gareth's discomfort. But before she had time to dwell any longer on her motives, chaos reigned. Several clients with their animals barged into the office, their dogs taking full advantage of the lull in the house.

'Reception is the door to your right,' Gareth ordered firmly, dragging his gaze from Melissa and turning his attention to the onlookers. 'Miss Moon will take your details.'

Gordon made a getaway and Gareth followed, but not without one last cursory glance at Melissa.

Rose, with a faint smile, patted her arm. 'Don't worry,' she advised softly, 'he's quite likeable when you get to know him!'

By mid-morning Melissa was wondering if she would ever get to know Gareth Tremaine.

The surgery was packed, one complaint after another, and a weimarana now lay dejectedly on the treatment-room floor. Gareth's attitude had been businesslike, and she was thankful for that. But his eyes regarded her from time to time with an expression she could only imagine was annoyance. Fuelled with irritation at her acquiescence with Rose, he probably suspected her of trying to edge her way in to cause trouble. And trouble she could cause, it was true.

Melissa looked away from the penetration of his gaze as she held the dog still. His fingers roamed the pearly mauve coat, examining with care a lump forming at the base of the neck. But his eyes travelled beyond the dog, whom he had already expertly assessed, and strayed to Melissa's face ... hoping, she imagined, for a sign on her part that she was not planning to raise the lid of his Pandora's box. Tempted to put his mind at rest, she teased herself with the idea of smiling coyly, an action any submissive partner in deception might take.

But she was not coy. And she was not submissive. Besides which, she hadn't asked him to kiss her!

'As far as I can see,' remarked Gareth edgily, looking up at the young lady owner, 'Jem has a snakebite. Don't worry... I'll give him an injection right away, but I rather think we're going to have to keep him in for observation.'

The young woman gulped back her apprehension. 'Is that really necessary? Can't I look after him at home?'

'It will be safer to have him here where I can keep an eye on him. If any danger signals arise, we can see them at once and act accordingly. But don't worry, there shouldn't be any. The bite just missed his windpipe – otherwise Jem might not be here to tell the tale.'

The girl nodded doubtfully and looked at Melissa. 'That's put me off bushy places and heathland for good. I can't understand how we didn't see it happen.'

Melissa took Jem's lead and coaxed the dog while Gareth gave him the injection. 'It's not your fault,' she told her comfortingly. 'Just a one-off. Luckily we've got it in time.'

When the girl had gone, Melissa took Jem to a recovery cage and made him comfortable, though his large, almond-shaped eyes searched the room for his mistress. 'Don't worry, Jem,' Melissa soothed in a soft voice, stroking him gently, 'you're going to be just fine.'

'I certainly hope so,' muttered Gareth. Soon he was down on his haunches beside her, staring at the dog. 'I expect you can see it's a severe bite... I think we'll start him off on a course of twenty-one two hundred and fifty milligrams of anti-inflammatory drugs. Then we shall have to drain the wound if it gets any worse.'

Melissa nodded, then flinched physically as his tough male thigh touched hers, almost overbalancing her with shock. Fighting the undeniable draw of attraction, she ordered her body to be sensible. No faint feelings, no hot flushes or trembling nerve-ends! But to her horror she developed a case of all three – and to a severe degree.

'I'll just get him some milk,' she heard herself saying, forcing her legs to straighten. But although she managed to stand up she was not quick enough to avoid a restraining hand on her arm.

'Melissa, forget about the milk, I want to talk to you.'

She turned to stare at him, alarmed by the instinctive response of her body to his touch. 'Yes ... what is it?'

Gareth shifted his gaze uneasily to the door. Obviously he didn't want to be disturbed when he tried to persuade her to reject Rose's plans. Melissa stood, knowing she was trembling from head to foot, unable to equate her body's unnatural reaction to a mere touch of a hand.

'You mentioned having a problem with your grandfather,' he said roughly, his eyes almost scorching her skin.

'No, I didn't say a problem. I said I wanted to talk to him. We always make a habit of talking over anything, especially when there's a major decision to be made.'

'So you call coming to stay here for a few days a major decision?' One dark eyebrow arched mockingly against tanned skin.

Melissa felt anger rise in her, swamping the sentiment she had allowed to sway her previously. 'It's the very least of my worries. As a favour to your parents, after all they've done for me, I'm only too happy to oblige.'

'I don't need a second housekeeper, if that's what you're thinking. I'm house-trained. I can boil an egg. And besides, the house won't be lacking a woman.'

It was said so easily that Melissa didn't know whether to laugh or to walk out of the room. Lacking a woman indeed! Was that really what was on his mind? The presence of a woman to make life easy for him, to pamper him, feed his ego, complete his sense of importance? Of all the conceited, self-centred people she had ever met in her life...

'Well? Now what's going around in that busy little mind of yours?' Gareth quipped icily. 'Look at me like that any longer and I shall turn to stone!'

'Impossible!' Melissa retorted, her voice husky with emotion. 'I doubt if anyone's stare – not even Medusa's – could affect you. It would have to penetrate that ego of yours before it got to flesh and bone. By which time I should think boredom would have overcome desire!'

Gareth opened his handsome mouth very slowly and then, to Melissa's humiliation, began to roar with laughter. Resting two very large elbows on the examination bench and chuckling still, he buried his head in his hands. Melissa found her eyes scouring the thick folds of dark brown hair untidily poking through strong male fingers. The humiliation at being the object of his mirth began to lessen as foolish sensations swept over her at the sound of the deep guttural voice, the ruffled hair, the long legs astride. Gulping back all she felt and trying to put a block on her thoughts, she muttered, 'And what, may I ask, do you find so funny?'

The man whose chiselled features were now softened by the relaxation of laughter pulled himself up to his full towering height. 'You, Melissa – I find you funny. And don't take that the wrong way … it's a very becoming quality, one a girl might give her eyeteeth for if she knew what it did to a man.'

'Then I'm glad I don't know,' observed Melissa. 'And I'm sorry to spoil your fun, but I think you're wanted…'

Gareth swivelled on his heel to find a large ruddy-faced gentleman standing at the door. 'When you've done, laddie, I'd take it as a favour if you'd see to my Alice outside. Can't bring her in – bladder's not what it should be.'

Gareth turned back to Melissa, a broad grin on his face and a look that melted every muscle in her body. 'I'll be back soon,' he told her. 'We'll finish our conversation later.'

Animals! thought Melissa, smiling to herself as she watched Gareth from the window, examining the full udder of a Toggenburg goat stubbornly refusing to move from the horsebox ramp on which it had marooned itself.

How she loved animals! And how Gareth did too. Nothing seemed beyond him when it came to an animal … even now he was stripping off his coat, rolling up shirtsleeves and gently massaging the distended teats of a testy-looking creature without giving a second thought to the idiotic forty-five-degree stance he and his patient were stuck at.

An hour later, after a successful draining off of milk, and Alice returned to her horsebox with a mouthful of garden elderberry, Gareth smoothed his dishevelled hair as he confronted the next patients, a cat and her four newly born kittens.

Melissa rallied to his side and to the continuing congestion of the day, since the Tremaines' attention was diverted to their packing and the practice left to fend for itself.

At five o'clock, Melissa closed the door and turned the key with a deep sigh of satisfaction. Somehow the day had come right as she intended it. Working with Gareth, she had to admit, had been both a pleasure and an insight. His way of doing things was different from his father's – not better, just different. More relaxed perhaps, but then he was the next generation and his calm disposition made it so easy to accept whatever trauma came along. With her head in the clouds she moved along the hall, only to hear the resonant echo of the grandfather clock on its last chime.

'Oh … goodness, no!' cried Melissa, staring at her watch in disbelief.

Gareth appeared, stretching his long body and easing off the white coat. 'Something wrong?' he queried.

'Er – no … well, yes. It's my grandfather. I was going to ask if I could leave early today. I'm supposed to pick him up at four-thirty from a senior citizens' club…'

'Hop in the Land Rover, I'll have you there in five minutes,' he said briskly.

'But I've got the Mini…'

'Do as you're told. That old heap of yours takes hours to warm up.'

And presently, though she tried her best to wriggle free of his suggestion, Melissa found herself being driven through Dorlington with Gareth whistling happily beside her and the awesome prospect lying ahead of Grampa's face when he saw who had come to collect him.

'Which is your grandfather?' asked Gareth, taking Melissa's arm as they crossed the busy road to the church hall. 'No, don't tell me. Let me spot the family resemblance.'

Melissa shuddered in anticipation. The very last thing she had wanted to happen was happening. Gareth had no place in her life, and yet here he was, propelling her across the road, the powerful fingers wrapped tightly around her arm, a grip that seemed to say … you're with me whether you like it or not!

'I ... I'll have to warn you,' she stammered, 'if Grampa puts up too much of a fight, then I'll order a taxi to take us home. It's not that he means to be difficult or rude, but he doesn't like change ... or new ideas...'

'Or new boyfriends?' Gareth glanced down at her as they came to a halt on the pavement.

'He knows all my friends well enough not to be alarmed,' she defended, 'but he might just get worried over a stranger's face.'

Gareth shrugged, impervious to her insinuation. 'I'll take the risk.'

Melissa peered through a glass partition into an almost empty building, feeling the fingers release her arm. In her confusion she might well have missed the small group of people gathered around a card table had not Gareth stopped her from hurrying away. 'Could that be him, down in the far corner?'

Melissa stared in disbelief. Grampa was absorbed in performing one of his ancient party tricks before a rapt audience. His fingers, usually so bent with arthritis, were turning the cards with surprising alacrity.

'Thank goodness for that!' breathed Melissa.

'Your grandfather is a lucky man to be so worried about,' Gareth said, his eyes gently assessing her.

Melissa laughed, tossing back her head of

fair hair, the late sun catching the hazel flecks in her grey eyes. 'I don't think he thinks that sometimes. I do tend to boss him about ... but just look at him! He seems so happy!'

'You can see why, can't you?' Gareth pointed to her grandfather's companion. 'Obviously the apple of that particular lady's eye, wouldn't you say?'

'I ... I can't believe it!' Melissa observed that the old man's attention was taken with a charming lady who sat beside him, so much so that he had obviously not noticed his transport was late!

'A good enough time as any for me to introduce myself,' Gareth told her, a grin glancing off his jaw. And in a matter of minutes he had introduced himself, explained their late arrival as his fault and charmingly swept her grandfather and the lady into the Land Rover.

Melissa found herself beside Mrs Purdy at the back. 'Your grandfather's a real breath of fresh air!' she declared in a youthful voice. 'We were both first-timers today, and to be honest we were determined not to like the club. But I can tell you it's the best day I've had in years. I can't wait for next Friday!'

'You're planning on going again?' Melissa asked in surprise.

'I certainly am! Your grandfather too. Wild horses wouldn't keep us away.' Faded blue eyes regarded Melissa from above rouged cheeks. 'You will let him come, won't you?'

'I doubt if I'd be able to stop him,' sighed Melissa as she listened to her grandfather's animated chatter in the front seat.

'Here we are,' announced Gareth as they arrived at Mrs Purdy's pretty bungalow in a quiet cul-de-sac.

'Thank you very much for the lift, dear,' said Mrs Purdy, bending forward and squeezing Gareth's broad shoulder. 'Will you all come in for a nice cup of tea?'

Melissa's refusal died on her lips as she watched her grandfather grapple with the handle of the door and with a swift wrist action swing it open. 'I'd love a cup of tea, Eileen. But we'll let these two young people get on their way, shall we? I'm sure we've taken up enough of their time.'

'But Gramps, what about your meal?'

'He can have his dinner here,' said Mrs Purdy with a smile. 'I do lovely apple pies and custard – Gusty's favourite.'

Melissa's bottom jaw dropped as she watched her grandfather wriggling himself out of the Land Rover. 'Don't worry about me, Melissa,' he said. 'Have fun with that young man of yours.'

Mrs Purdy looked back through the open window. 'Come and collect him about ten, if that's all right. I promise I'll take good care of him – and enjoy yourself, dear ... as if you

120

wouldn't with such a charming fellow as your Gareth!'

'He's not my–' began Melissa, only to find she was talking to thin air. The couple, arms linked, disappeared into the bungalow without even so much as a wave goodbye.

'Don't look so worried, Melissa,' murmured Gareth as he turned on the engine. 'They can be forgiven for their mistake, don't you think?'

'What mistake?' asked Melissa, staring at the empty pavement.

'It's obvious, isn't it?' Gareth swung the Land Rover round a sharp bend. 'They've jumped to the wrong conclusion ... that you and I are lovers.'

Only the green slant of laughing eyes stopped her from replying. Instead she gulped back the insane thoughts that crowded her mind and prayed that the flush on her cheeks was not as severe as the whirring, nonsensical beating of her palpitating heart.

CHAPTER SIX

Lovers.

The word rippled through her mind.

It came again as she tried to sleep that night.

Lovers...! Melissa closed her eyes, her damp body lying hot and restless between the sheets.

Lovers meant people in love, people like her parents whom she cherished as role models. They had loved, she was sure of that. Even the faintest recollection of them was shot through with a gentleness and closeness she knew could only be love. Their early death had preserved this certainty for her, for how could any heavenly hand ever separate such a love?

'That's what I want,' Melissa told herself softly, burying her face in the pillow, her damp skin clinging to the cotton. And, she promised herself in the hazy moment just before sleep, she would never settle for less.

'A long trip,' Gareth murmured as though to himself.

The tail lights of the red Toyota, his father's car, flashed a last goodbye at the end of the drive.

'Sensible, though, to break the journey in Cumbria,' Melissa said, forcing her attention on the vehicle, resolving that she would stay exactly where she was on the porch and not move as Gareth drew closer. She was not afraid to be alone with him. Of course she wasn't! If she had ever doubted her motives she would never have agreed to moving in while Gordon and Rose were away. Besides, Dian and Peter were due back this afternoon, and what could possibly happen while they were in the house?

'I would have preferred to see them use the Land Rover,' said Gareth, digging his hands in his pockets and catching her briefly with his arm. This slight collision caused her over-aware skin to react violently, goose bumps littering her arms and legs.

'Your father's been longing to try the car out,' Melissa said, rallying her senses. 'Whenever he gets a spare moment he's in the garage talking to it the way most people talk to their plants.'

The last ribbon of exhaust curled up into the pine trees and the little red dot passed out of sight. The Tremaines were gone, and the place seemed strangely quiet without them.

Gareth moved closer. 'It's a funny thing, the way you talk about my parents. I get the feeling you know them better than I do.'

'They're nice people,' Melissa said thought-fully. 'In fact, they're the nicest people I know … apart from Gramps, of course.'

With that curious expression on his face, was it possible he suspected her of being an opportunist as she herself had suspected him? The argument, if it was one, could certainly go both ways, particularly as Gordon had always imagined his only son lost to the other side of the world – what was so unusual about gaining a daughter to fill his place?

But his expression was implacable; if anything, the eyes regarded her quizzically.

'You've been away five years,' Melissa stressed, looking under her thick lashes at him. 'You'll need time to readjust.'

'That's a polite way of saying you think I've been too heavy-handed since I've come home.' Gareth gave her a humourless smile. 'One of the things I'm having to get used to is the way English people wrap up what they want to say in layers of what's irrelevant just to make themselves sound polite. In Australia, there's no beating about the bush, if you'll excuse the pun. Maybe it's the weather … the heat that drives people into being pretty honest about what they feel.'

'And you think an English person isn't?'

'Hey!' exclaimed Gareth, laughing, his mood changing quickly. Removing his hands from his pockets, he placed them squarely on Melissa's arms and gave her a playful shake. 'Come on, now! My folks are only just gone and I've brought an icy glint to those lovely grey eyes. Remember, you and I are going to have to look after this place together ... try as I might to get you out of the job.'

Nine o'clock on a Saturday morning, thought Melissa, struggling under the effect of the hands, and I feel almost delirious just because he's behaving so nicely! 'I really had no option other than to help,' she said in a softer tone. 'Your parents ask so little of me...'

'And you felt you couldn't refuse.'

'Yes, I suppose so.'

His hands dropped away from her and he shrugged. 'Well, aren't I the lucky man? Whatever lamp I rubbed, I seemed to have materialised the right genie ... bumping into you last Sunday was no accident, then. Shall we call it destiny?'

Melissa avoided the probing eyes, the gaze which defied her to remember last week and their first meeting. She wanted to keep her feet planted firmly on the ground, and when her mind roved over the mental picture of those long legs sticking out from the Mini, the green eyes gazing down at her as she treated Flash, she seemed to lose all hope of thinking rationally. Like last night, when her rebellious thoughts had surfaced in the form of tantalising dreams...

'I'd better check the dogs,' she decided, making her way to the inner glass door and into the hall.

'Jem's wound's coming to a head!' Gareth shouted after her. 'I changed his dressings earlier. Oh, and we won't have to worry about Flash, he'll be going this morning.'

Melissa came to a grinding halt. 'Going?' She turned back to stare at him. 'Do you mean ... to a kennels?'

'If you'll give me five minutes...' Gareth searched in the hall cupboard, retrieving his white coat.

'But you said a few days ago ... we wouldn't! You said we'd keep him until he was a hundred per cent!'

'That was a few days ago ... circumstances have changed.' Gareth pulled on his coat and ran a large hand through unruly dark hair.

'How can they have changed? How?' Melissa asked angrily. 'He's still recovering. You know what happens when they go in kennels ... you know it's traumatic for them!'

'Calm down, calm down,' he told her steadily as he walked past her into the treatment-room. 'You really will have to keep a check on that temper of yours, my girl. Look before you leap! Now, if you'll give me a chance, I'll explain.'

But he was never given the chance. The phone began its usual tirade, and by the time Melissa had finished answering it he was fully occupied in his room.

At a quarter to one, when it was time for her to close the door for the half-day, Melissa had stirred herself into a paroxysm of resentment. How dared Gareth get rid of the dog she had knocked down – and at the moment his father's back was turned? Was he doing it out of spite, to get back at her for moving in? If so, it was the very lowest of reprisals. Gordon would never have done such a thing ... he would have tried every avenue until he found a home for Flash. She couldn't believe Gareth would do this just to spite her!

Her cheeks were burning with a rosy anger when Mr Tubbs walked into Reception. She had to make a concerted effort to put a hold on the little speech she was preparing in her mind. It had many clauses to it ... her suspicions and her conclusions, for instance, all melted together with a fair sprinkling of home truths.

'Hello, Melissa.' Mr Tubbs stood before her, turning the hat in his hands. 'Gareth about?'

'He's just finishing with his last client,' Melissa answered, thinking Mr Tubbs was going to be disappointed if he had come to take the dog for a walk. How was Gareth going to break the news to him, or was he indifferent to the old man's feelings?

A fresh wave of anger surfaced as she watched the diminutive figure take a seat in the waiting-room. How could Gareth do it? How could he?

'Melissa?' Gareth stood in the hall beckoning her. Reluctantly she put down her pen, tidied her papers with an extra flourish, demonstrating her disapproval, and slowly walked out to meet him. 'What in heaven's name is the matter with you?' he asked in a whispered tone.

'What exactly do you think? You've avoided me all the morning, and I know why. I just can't believe that you'd consider Flash going into kennels!'

Gareth squared his broad shoulders, small red dots of anger colouring his cheeks. 'I've got a client I'd like you to talk to. She's upset and doesn't want to leave her dog with us. But there are some tests I've got to run and I'd like him in until Monday. Do you think you could possibly persuade her ... bearing in mind your skills with Mrs Stroud?'

'If you're doing this deliberately, Gareth—'

'I'm doing my job – which is more than you seem to be at the moment, Melissa. Now, will you do as I ask, please?'

Feeling as though she could willingly strangle her boss, Melissa turned towards the treatment-room. By the time she had discovered the woman and her beagle and talked over the problem, her anger had ripened to fresh proportions. Gareth was purposely making it difficult for her. He knew she opposed the idea of Flash going! It was the one way he could effectively get back at her. It was mean, it was petty and it was childish – and what was more, she was going to tell him so!

Melissa took the beagle to a recovery cage and settled him. The house seemed strangely quiet … both Gareth and Mr Tubbs were nowhere to be seen. He had probably sent the poor old chap off without a moment's prick of conscience.

Going to bolt the front door, Melissa peered through the glass. A small figure bobbed down the path. Attached to the figure was a lead … and to the lead, a dog.

She swung the door open and ran out into the fresh May air. 'Mr Tubbs!' she called, and, running to the dog, bent down and buried her face in the sweet-smelling coat. 'You're taking him?'

The elderly man smiled, his face lighting up as he saw her. 'I would have waited to say goodbye, but you were busy. Gareth said to call in next week with him.'

'But how?' persisted Melissa.

'Didn't Gareth say?'

She shook her head, receiving a healthy paw in her hand as she listened.

'That young man, he's a real brick! Done it all for me – injections, the mange stuff, even delivered me a huge sack of dry food. And I'm to bring Flash in for treatment whenever I like and Gareth said the charge will be minimal.' Mr Tubbs drew a gnarled hand over the rich, fluffy fur. 'I said I'd try to pay him back, but he won't hear of it.'

Melissa stood up and felt a little shiver go along her spine as she realised how wrong she had been to prejudge Gareth. 'I had no idea you were having him, Mr Tubbs,' she said.

'He said to keep it under my hat. Said Flash was sort of special.'

'Yes, he is special, that's quite true,' Melissa agreed thoughtfully. Did Gareth really think of Flash as special? Sentimental as it was, there was a little place in her heart reserved for the animal who had first brought them together in such an unusual way. It was probably stupid to think Gareth thought the same, but might he? Now Flash was going to a good home, to be cared for by a responsible person, and Gareth had made it all possible...

Mr Tubbs cheerfully waved goodbye. Melissa locked the front door, slowly turning the key. If she had just given Gareth time to explain instead of jumping to the wrong conclusions! Humble pie, she thought meekly. Oh, dear, she would have to eat it – and rather a large portion too. Why, oh, why had she been so impetuous? Her old enemy back again, as Gramps would say.

'Oh, well, I might as well get it over with,' she sighed. Softly as she checked the rooms. There was computing to be finished, but as she was staying here, she could work at her own speed. Jem and the beagle were comfortable in their cages and from the window Beetle was scoffing a mountain of food. But no Gareth ... was he sulking? Was he waiting for the piece of humble pie to be served on a silver platter?

Melissa stopped to freshen up in the downstairs cloakroom, postponing the inevitable and rehearsing a new speech, one with an apology in it. Tracing a hint of lipstick on her lips and brushing her thick hair into a shining halo, she tried a contrite expression in the mirror and, failing miserably, went off in search of Gareth.

The search didn't take long.

The man's stomach had led him to the place of refreshment, to Mrs Carter's thoughtful packing of a salad and cold meats in the refrigerator. He had spread the feast on the table, set places for two and poured fruit juice.

'Welcome!' He gave her a disarming smile and gestured to a seat.

'You've been busy.' Melissa sat at the table and looked up at him.

'You're worth it. You managed the beagle

lady, didn't you?' The smile spread into a mischievous grin and he added, 'And by the looks of you you're not angry any more. Does that mean I can eat?'

'I saw Mr Tubbs,' said Melissa, watching the long, firm legs thread themselves under the table, making her heart twitch and tumble as she spoke. 'And it seems I was a little hasty.' She hurried on, words flowing in explanation. Finally, defeated by his silence, she ended, 'It's just that I couldn't bear to see him go to kennels!'

'Did you think I could?' Gareth picked up the salad and offered it to her, the diamonds of green glinting reproachfully from their sockets. 'Now eat and be quiet. Then we'll get your case from the Mini... I presume you brought luggage?'

'Just an overnight bag, a few things.'

'Not planning on staying long?' Gareth filled his own plate to mountainous proportions. 'Afraid the big bad wolf might come and knock on your bedroom door?'

Melissa raised her eyes, a smile edging her lips as she studied him sitting contentedly in his seat enjoying his game. 'If he did come and knock, no amount of huffing and puffing would blow the door down,' she parried with daintily raised eyebrows. 'This particular Red Riding Hood has had the presence of mind to build her house with bricks and mortar. In Australia, I understand, they're not quite so resilient.'

Gareth's smile broke into the widest of grins. Throwing back his dark head, he gave vent to the beautiful sound that so attracted her: his laughter. It was spontaneous and free and mirrored a feeling deep inside her, a feeling no other human being had been able to incite. She began to laugh too, watching the sensual parting of his lips as his mirth filled the kitchen. It was as though she was being taken over by the sight and sound and the presence of him … and wondrously it felt right … perfectly right. If there was just an ounce of sincerity in those twinkling eyes … she felt, for the moment, she would be happy.

Yes, while she was here, in his home, sharing the air he breathed, she would be happy.

'I thought you said just an overnight bag?' Gareth hauled Melissa's suitcase from the back of the Mini. 'What have you got in it … rocks?'

'Just a few changes.' Melissa grabbed a holdall and her bag.

'Never known a woman who could travel lightly,' Gareth volunteered as he slammed the car door.

'How much of the female population of Australia does that apply to?' Melissa asked lightly. 'Seventy-five per cent, or am I underestimating you?'

He manoeuvred the case into the house and dropped it at the foot of the stairs. 'Your sense of humour matches your freckles – did you know that? It lights up when warmed ... and by the looks of it I'm warming both nicely.'

Melissa stood in the hall clutching her bags and wishing she weren't so transparent. Little did he know just how much he warmed her, her body beginning to stir with unfamiliar sensations as she struggled to find an answer. Trying to hide her inner dilemma, she looked up at Gareth, murmuring, 'Shall we go?'

'Lead on – or rather lead up ... you do know which room you're in?'

Melissa cast her eyes to the ground, turning her face away from the eyes which were already silently teasing her because somehow he seemed to sense just how nervous she felt walking up the stairs with him. 'Your mother showed me before she went,' she responded lightly, forcing herself to sound as though she hadn't a care in the world. 'Dian and Peter are in the guest bedrooms; I'm occupying the room on the next floor.'

'Opposite me.'

Melissa bit her bottom lip, knowing very well Rose had positioned her opposite Gareth. 'It has a telephone,' she explained, 'for evening calls.'

Gareth followed her up the red-carpeted staircase, making light work of the heavy luggage. 'Wonderful, these old Victorian houses, aren't they? So much space ... one can almost get lost in them. In fact, calling from the top floor here, you'd have a job to hear down there.'

Melissa stopped at the white-painted door she knew was hers. 'Thank you,' she said, tilting up her chin, deliberately ignoring the insinuation. 'I can manage the case now.'

'Always independent ... you should have that as your motto!' Gareth dropped the case and reached past her to open the door. 'My job isn't finished yet ... and I intend to finish it, to make you properly welcome.'

'That really isn't necessary, Gareth–' she began.

'Just follow me.' He ushered her firmly into the sun-filled room. 'Fresh towels, clean sheets, a little fresh air too...' Moving towards the sash window, he raised it a fraction, dropping back the pure white nets.

Melissa gazed around the room, remembering it from last year when she had stayed while Gordon recovered from flu. Dusted in magnolia, the room held Rose's delicate touch – white-painted dainty furniture, rosebud curtains and a thick pale carpet. The door swung open behind her and she looked around. The door opposite was

Gareth's ... the door she had often wondered about, the room that had always been Gareth's, the elusive son who had gone to seek his fortune in another land, the land of milk and honey.

'Yes, I'm just a shout away, as you can see.'

Melissa swung back to face him, and her heart plummeted as she saw he had moved from the window and lazed on the bed. 'Very comfortable!' He pushed the deep divan with his strong fingers and the duvet sprang bouncily back. 'Just testing,' he drawled slowly, raising his eyes to meet hers.

'I ... I think I can test it for myself,' Melissa said hoarsely, feeling as though she had just stepped from a fairground switch-back. 'Hadn't you better check the answer-phone?'

'No need,' Gareth told her, his gaze mocking. 'I've asked Walter to take the weekend calls ... he'll get in contact if there's anything he can't handle.'

'But that's what I'm here for ... the telephone – any emergencies,' insisted Melissa, refusing to return the mischievous twinkle in Gareth's eye.

'Have you forgotten tonight?' He arched his dark brows. 'Your date with Peter? Someone has to take calls.'

She stiffened, remembering the rash promise she had made to Peter. 'You mean the four of us,' she corrected, thinking the arrangement sounded safer in numbers.

'I didn't read it like that.'

'Peter simply asked us out to be polite. He's that sort of person,' she explained.

'Really? Woman's intuition on your part?'

Melissa dumped her bags angrily on the floor. 'I don't know what we're discussing Peter for–'

'Nor do I,' interrupted Gareth, beaming her a roguish smile. He patted the space beside him. 'Come and talk to me. Give me five minutes of your valuable time.'

Melissa stared at the bed, at Gareth's innocent expression, and felt her body going rigid in anticipation. It was sheer madness, feeling this aware of him, she thought, panic-stricken.

Gareth gave a sharp, unnerving laugh. 'You're not afraid to accept a date from a total stranger, but you're afraid to sit for five minutes beside a working colleague. I wouldn't have had you down for a coward, Melissa.'

His accusation made her deeply aware of the silence permeating the house and of the three flights of stairs she would have to run to get to the bottom – if need be. But it was ridiculous to think along those lines … he was just bluffing, belittling her. Well, she would show him she was no coward, nor was she subject to emotional blackmail, no matter how cloaked it appeared to be.

She moved across the room, aware of his eyes following her. Sitting on the edge of the large, comfortable bed, she began huskily, 'You're provoking me, Gareth, aren't you? You're making fun of me. And perhaps you've a right to ... me coming to stay here like this... I know you didn't want it. I know you think I might be trouble ... telling Dian, for instance...'

'It did occur to me.' Gareth moved up the bed towards her, his large body indenting the duvet considerably. 'And would you – tell Dian?'

Melissa gasped as she felt his hands travel the contours of her forearms, coming to rest on the downy curve of her upper arms as he bent his head to one side, his green eyes drowning her, anaesthetising her mind and body as though she had been given a drug. 'Will you tell?'

'W-why should I?' she stammered in a small voice, as she watched the black pupils expand hypnotically. His gaze slowly slipped downwards, travelled from the point of her small nose, to her well-defined lips, quivering now. She ran her pink tongue over them, wetting them, feeling as though for years she had been stranded in a desert.

'My ... impetuous little English rose!' he breathed. And for one heart-tilting second she thought he would kiss her. Instead, his hand reached up to her chin and took it

138

bringing her closer. Her body arched involuntarily towards him. There was nothing she could do to stop herself, no power on earth could break the spell he had cast, mesmerising her, drawing her closer and making her yield to him.

'Close your eyes,' she heard him whisper softly.

To her astonishment, she found herself obeying him. It was as though her will had been taken from her, to be replaced by a burning sensation that consumed her mind and body. As though by some wizardry his touch had captured the moment and forced it to stand still – as she herself was still, enraptured by the sound of his voice, the touch of his hand, the musky odour of his body. As though all her life she had been waiting for this one moment.

And then his lips came down on hers, softly at first as though she might have stepped unsuspecting into a spider's web. The memory of the garden filled her mind, as the web seemed to catch across her eyelids and her eyelashes. The sun sparkling through the trees, the heavy scent of leaves piled on leaves waiting crustily to be burnt.

Her arms travelled upwards, her fingers roved his hair, caressing the strong arch of his neck. With senses spinning she traced with her fingertips the slight, soft indentation of his neck muscle. Her ears drummed with the echo of her heartbeat as the slow kiss transformed itself into a demanding, desperate action. Suddenly ... and she had no conception how ... her body seemed to be melting into his, her hands running over the hard line of his shoulders down to the sharp and animal-like curve of his spine.

'My darling girl!' His breath stroked her cheek as every movement of his body rippled beneath her fingertips as he spoke. She tasted the salt on his lips, filling her with an insurmountable desire to return the generous probing of the sweet, delicious mouth. The flickering sensation of his tongue told her he wanted more and he demanded it straight away!

Did he know just exactly what he was doing to her, a man of his obvious experience with dozens of women? Was she just another body to be caressed, another woman to add to his list of conquests?

'Relax...' he whispered in the same tone as he had told her to close her eyes. 'Don't fight me, Melissa, you're not really a fighter.'

She felt the instinctive and logical recoil of her intellectual mind – but her body did not, could not, follow its example. It was sinking deeper into the illusion that she was part of him. As her eyelids flickered open, sunlight skimmed his face, showing the ragged skin so masculine in its texture, the jade colouring of his eyes turning to emerald. He kissed her again, before she had time to murmur, to breathe, to protest.

Finally she allowed herself a response, silencing the nagging voice that drowned in the heat of her excitement. His skin burnt against hers, her body trembled and stiffened and arched as he held her closer, lost as they were in the folds of the bed. 'I want you, Melissa, I need you...'

In answer, she allowed his hand to travel over the fine material of her uniform, skimming the hard buds of her breasts. Soon the fingers forced themselves to disentangle the buttons and reach hot, damp skin beneath.

'God in heaven, Melissa, you're beautiful...' The words ricocheted in her brain. She had never thought of herself as beautiful, never imagined someone saying those words with such conviction, yet here she was, allowing herself to fall – and to fall headlong – into the riskiest proposition because of an attraction that was purely chemistry. What motive could he possibly have for making love to her other than a transient physical need?

Four little letters made her stay the fingers at her breast.

Dian.

Dian's face ... now that was a beautiful face. Delicate, fine-boned, with those large eyes ... eyes which ought to be keeping a better check on the man whom she had followed across the world. Perhaps that was the way Gareth planned it ... playing one woman off against the other?

Suddenly Melissa sat up, stunned by the conviction that she was being bewitched somehow by Gareth as he almost ferried her across the breathless threshold she had always promised herself would be special, simply magic. She longed for him. The fact that he was a man devoted to chasing money and women had not prevented her from almost allowing him to make love to her.

'Now what's wrong?' Gareth's voice came roughly as he gripped her by the wrist.

'Everything,' bleated Melissa, trying to pull her hand free. 'Let go of me, Gareth!'

'Not until you tell me why. Seconds ago you were crying out to be held... I didn't imagine that response of yours!'

'I don't care what you thought ... you're a fast worker, aren't you? So considerately giving me the benefit of the afternoon before Dian comes back. Is that why you had the phone conveniently switched through to Walter?'

'You little witch!' exclaimed Gareth, struggling with her as she tried to get up from the bed. 'Your mind's certainly been working overtime – even when I was kissing you!'

'And I wonder where your mind was!'

Melissa cried angrily, lunging at him with her free hand.

'You're a tease, do you know that?' He was up, pulling her with him, shaking her. 'Do you know that?'

Watching the rise and fall of the powerful chest, whorls of dark hair rising provocatively from the open shirt, the shirt which had come apart in the tussle on the bed, Melissa was aware of her own desperate attraction to him, so desperate that even now she could fall helplessly into his arms ... if she allowed herself. In vain she tried to push him away.

'You've met your match this time,' she heard him whisper raggedly as the high colour in his cheeks accentuated the blazing green of his determined gaze. 'You let me hold you ... touch you ... don't you know you were asking me to make love to you?'

Melissa savagely twisted her arms, heard her own strangled cry as she thrust away from him. 'That's ridiculous! Do you think every woman is going to fall at your feet? Do you think I'm going to let you make love to me just because you kissed me?'

Gareth pulled her back to him, encircling her with his arms so she could not move. Tensing her body and biting back a gasp, she glared at him defiantly, though every part of her being yearned inwardly for him, causing a physical torrent of pain to encompass her.

'It wasn't just a kiss, was it?' he demanded in a deep voice. 'Answer me, Melissa – and truthfully!'

For what seemed an eternity Melissa faltered on the brink of an abyss. A dark and cavernous drop lay beneath her, the abyss of admitting her own emotions to someone who might push her over the brink, never to see her again. Should he reach out and capture her before she fell, it would be a miracle. And miracles were scarcities these days, she thought in a turmoil of indecision. But what if she gave him the chance of her truth? What if she admitted to her growing need of him, to the sensations that were gripping the lower half of her body with a relentless determination? Only she knew … only she could tell him … should she?

From somewhere in the distance a car sounded its horn. The small sound, so un-real compared to the singing in her ears and the pounding of her crazed heart, had little effect on her.

But when Gareth released her, the warmth of his body drawing away from her own life force, she knew the moment of truth had passed. Desperately she fought back a painful disappointment as he walked to the window, glancing down into the car park.

'You're a very lucky girl.' Gareth cast his eyes back to her, a look of contempt masking his face. 'Your date has arrived.' Walking brusquely out of the room, he looked briefly back. 'And I should be careful if I were you when you turn on the charm for Peter. He's a hell of a big guy – and Australians, as I warned you, are inclined to take a person literally. Perhaps that's something you ought to consider before you let him take you to bed.'

CHAPTER SEVEN

Melissa was so furious, if she'd had something that was hers to throw she would have thrown it.

There was a delightful jug and hand basin perching on the tallboy, but it was too good to waste on a conceited, arrogant, self-centred chauvinist like Gareth Tremaine!

Instead, Melissa strode to the window, fuming. From behind the curtain she saw Dian and Peter clambering out of their hire-car. A third figure strode into the car park, and Melissa held her breath as she eavesdropped, a few phrases filtering in through the open window.

'Darling, I've missed you so much...' The willowy brunette threw herself into Gareth's unresisting arms. 'Have you missed me?'

Melissa flattened herself on the wall beside the window. Gareth's voice was too low to interpret, but the greeting Dian had given him wasn't!

'Perhaps that's something you ought to consider before you let Peter take you to bed...' Melissa's cheeks flushed angrily as she thought of Gareth's infuriating last remark. He had obviously never doubted from the start that she was his own for the taking whenever he wanted her, and when she'd objected he'd probably been unable to reconcile that enormous ego of his!

Peter's voice drifted up, breaking into Melissa's angered concentration. 'Don't forget tonight, Gareth... I thought we might give one of the casinos a look-over. OK by you and Melissa?'

'...no problem as far as I'm concerned, but you'd better see Melissa for yourself.'

Melissa flopped on to the bed dejectedly. What was she supposed to do now, for heaven's sake? She felt a complete fool for allowing Gareth to make a pass – and a pass that seemed to work very well too, the memory of his featherlight touch making her shiver from head to toe.

Gramps had always told her she hadn't mixed enough with people of her own age ... perhaps he was right. The effect Gareth was having on her was almost as ridiculous as the crush she'd had in her teens on the school biology master, with his mysterious aloofness and outlandish horn-rimmed glasses. The phase had passed – not without a lot of book-dropping and knee-trembling, but it had passed – just as this one would over Gareth, Melissa told herself resolutely, feeling better.

'Don't panic,' she ordered herself. 'Show him you're not the gauche, naïve little thing he imagines you to be! And don't do anything rash like handing in your notice – or opting out of having fun with perfectly nice people!'

An ordinary boyfriend, that was what she needed, a luxury she had never seemed to have time for, someone with their feet firmly planted on the ground, someone down-to-earth.

'Melissa?' A down-to-earth, ordinary voice broke circumspectly into her thoughts.

She sprang up guiltily to see Peter standing in her open bedroom door. 'Peter! How .. how are you?' she asked him.

'Great ... a bit groggy from the drive, but I'll get my head down later. Are you busy?'

'No ... no, not at all.'

Peter raised two large bushy eyebrows, displaying very extraordinary blue eyes beneath. 'Look, don't mind me asking, but I reckon Gareth didn't seem too sure about you coming tonight. I thought I'd try to persuade you myself.'

'I don't need any persuading, Peter, I'm looking forward to a night out,' Melissa said, surprised at her own confident tone. Maybe this friendly, easygoing young man might provide just the right distraction – in spite of Gareth's barbed warning.

Peter smiled his appreciation, looking ruggedly handsome in his jeans and white T-shirt which showed off his corn-coloured tan to perfection. She could do a lot worse than enjoy Peter's stay in England.

'You're moving in while the Tremaines are away?' he asked.

'Yes, that's right. I stayed for a while last year, actually. Gordon had a bad bout of flu and Rose needed a hand.'

Peter nodded, staring at her wistfully, not overstepping the boundaries of her bed-room door. 'I wish I had a girl like you to rely on back home. I'm desperate for a good secretary in our Melbourne office. The oil business is pretty lucrative, you know.'

Melissa laughed shyly. Peter was a nice guy; perhaps if he were based in England she might have applied for the job. But her heart was set on animals, nothing could ever take their place, even if he did work over here. 'I'm sure you've got dozens of girls lining up for the vacancy!'

'No one like you. Ever thought about a trip to Oz?'

Melissa was about to answer that she

never had when Gareth's face loomed in the background, giving her heart a jolt.

'Trying to talk our staff into swapping sides?' he asked humourlessly.

'Can you blame me?' Peter replied laconically, turning to face him. 'Don't mind me, Gareth, she wouldn't come anyway.'

Gareth shrugged, his lithe and muscular body six inches taller than the substantial Peter. Melissa wished she didn't have to look at him, for her mind was still running riot over what had happened between them, but much to her dismay Gareth looked as if he had totally forgotten the incident, casually discussing the arrangements for the evening.

'About eight, then,' Gareth finished, slowly moving across the hall to his room. 'We'll have a bite to eat first, then go on to the Blue Moon. How does that suit you?'

'Fair enough.' Peter gave her a friendly wink over his shoulder. 'Better watch out, Melissa, your feet won't touch the ground tonight!'

She watched the impressive body slowly move off like a large, lumbering bear, comfortable and easy in its slow stride, leaving her to face the picture of suspicion across the hall, Gareth with his hands dug deeply in his pockets staring at her accusingly.

'You needn't look at me like that, Gareth Tremaine,' she hissed tartly, and with her heart thumping like a drum she closed the door with a bang, much harder than she really meant.

He was impossible! Absolutely impossible!

Men! thought Melissa angrily, birds of a feather. But then why should she worry? She had no intention whatsoever of spoiling Gareth's relationship with Dian, in spite of whatever it was his devious mind was brewing up – and she didn't want a serious relationship with Peter either, and Peter felt the same about her, she was sure. It was just Gareth's look that disturbed her ... passing judgement with those accusing green eyes of his. Well, he would have to think what he liked! Tonight she was going to enjoy herself!

Melissa locked the shower-room door firmly – and then bolted it, just in case.

She had managed to avoid everyone during the afternoon, slipping out only to walk Susie and check the dogs.

She ran the hot water over her face and body, relaxing her taut muscles while she thought of what she should wear. She had packed a pretty pale pink dress in a silky soft material and a black designer suit in case of emergencies, though it would probably suit a funeral far more than an evening out on the town, she thought wryly. After scenting herself, adding a luxurious softener to her hair rinse and letting her silvery fair locks dry naturally on her shoulders, she decided on the pink.

Her reflection pleased her as she stood in her bedroom before the long mirror: small waist accentuating the subtly cut dress, curves gentle and flowing under the clinging material. Unlike Dian with her boyish hips, Melissa's hourglass figure looked its best in the simplest of fashions. Her shoulders were bare, touched delicately by dainty pink straps, the scalloped neckline sheltering firm, round breasts. She threaded opalescent earrings through her lobes and crimped her halo of silvery fair hair as a last discerning touch.

'Wow!' Peter whistled as she walked down the stairs. He stood waiting for her in the hall beneath as the grandfather clock struck eight. 'And a lady who's on time too!'

As she moved into his open arms he gave her a playful kiss. 'Can't resist you,' he said teasingly.

Melissa warmed to the outgoing Australian for his consideration in making her feel at ease. 'You look very impressive indeed,' she told him admiringly, casting approving eyes over the fawn suit hanging rangily from well developed limbs. 'I can tell you've been shopping … Oxford Street, maybe?'

Peter grinned. 'Dian dragged me round London till I bought something. Said she was fed up with seeing me in jeans and sneakers!'

She smiled at the friendly, admiring face. He was not a vain man, and she liked that. He was kind and thoughtful and possessed a superb sense of fun. If she tried very hard, she might just be able to transfer her idiot feelings to someone who deserved them!

'You two haven't taken long in getting to know one another.' Dian's frosty tones startled Melissa into taking a step back from Peter. 'Melissa, you really will have to give my brother time to get his breath … he's hardly been in England a few days!'

Melissa's grey eyes sprang open at the vision descending the stairs. No wonder Gareth, following behind, could hardly keep his eyes off her! Dian looked stunning in a pencil-slim black dress – what there was of it – boasting a daring neckline and scooped back.

'I was admiring your brother's choice in English clothes,' said Melissa, trying to recover her equilibrium, feeling a bit like a country bumpkin in Dian's sultry shadow.

'Not his choice,' Dian responded, 'mine. Peter's useless with clothes.'

''Fraid so,' agreed Peter with a concili-atory smile at Melissa. 'Dian's the one with the dress sense. Left to me, I'd have picked something a lot less flashy.'

'Flashy!' cooed Dian. 'You'd still be in your oil-rig gear if I'd allowed it!' Then, as if just remembering Gareth was there, she turned and linked a slender arm through his. 'Now, you two, where are you going to take us? Somewhere special, I hope?'

Melissa watched the piercing ebony eyes flicker over Gareth, dressed in an immaculate dark suit that emphasised every inch of his slim-hipped athletic build. But Dian seemed to be much too conscious of her own good looks to notice – perhaps a legacy of her modelling career with the attention of the crowd always firmly fixed on her? But to Melissa's rising irritation Dian's teasing allure had apparently captivated Gareth, who hadn't uttered a word!

'Your department, this, Gareth,' said Peter lightly.

Gareth seemed suddenly to come to life. 'I saw a new Italian restaurant advertised last night, on the coast. Then I thought the Blue Moon Club and casino. It's years since I've been there, but we can try it if you like.'

For the first time his eyes lingered on Melissa. She tried to look away, but found the exquisite pleasure of having his attention on her was too much to give up. Every instinct in her body replayed the treacherous sentiments which had beset her a few hours ago. She had promised herself that nothing was going to get in the way of her enjoyment of the evening, yet the unnerving glint in those greeny eyes was already making nonsense of her secret vow.

'Any objections, Melissa?' Gareth asked lightly, warming her senses with his voice.

'Of course she hasn't!' Peter answered smoothly for her. 'We're going to have a real party tonight ... aren't we, my sweet?'

Dian eyed her brother with a less than friendly glance. 'Our car or the Land Rover, Gareth?'

'I don't think you'd find the Land Rover terribly comfortable.' Gareth wrapped a dress scarf gently around her slender, bare shoulders.

Melissa, feeling a grinding pain in her chest, silently allowed herself to be ushered out into the night, telling herself she wasn't in the least bothered that Gareth's fingers seemed to linger far too long on the naked shoulders.

Sitting in the front seat of the luxurious BMW, next to Peter, who drove, Melissa heard snippets of conversation from the back seat. Dian was telling Gareth how she had been booked by the modelling agency in the city, winning a contract with an élite swimwear firm who had promised her dazzling assignments.

Gareth's responsive laughter was beginning – just – to get on her nerves. If she was listening to his conversation then he certainly was not bothered about hers!

'Take the next on the left, Peter,' Gareth

called from the back, deigning to interrupt his dialogue with Dian. 'As far as I can remember, the road forks quite sharply.'

Ristorante Napoli was a pretty place; small round tables decorated with the traditional bottles of lighted candlewax, soft, harmonious music in the background coupled with swift, attentive waiters, a bottle of sparkling house wine, pasta smothered in a delicious sauce and mouth-watering chilled desserts comprised a superb meal.

'I feel lucky tonight,' said Peter at last, finishing every scrap. 'Must be you, Melissa ... you're going to be my rabbit's foot on the casino tables!'

Dian, who was sitting next to Gareth, daintily picking at her food, raised a doubting eyebrow. 'You always feel lucky, Peter. You never feel any different.'

Instantly sorry for the big Australian, who seemed to take all his sister's gibes with a good-natured grin, Melissa said defensively, 'I've a feeling your brother is going to be just that extra extra bit lucky tonight!'

'That's my girl!' expostulated Peter, leaning across the table to pick up her hand and plant a substantial kiss on it. 'I need all the sympathy I can get...'

'I don't believe a word of it,' parried Melissa, her eyes telling Peter she was enjoying the teasing, leaving her hand to be fondled as he acted the fool.

'You're wise not to believe him,' Dian cut in quickly, disapproval tingeing her tone. 'My brother has always been able to elicit people's sympathy ... don't let that look of angelic innocence fool you.'

Melissa raised her chin a fraction, aware of Gareth's quiet scrutiny. 'I'll keep it in mind,' she answered lightly, secretly thinking Dian was offering sour grapes simply because the attention, for once, was not focused on her.

'If everyone is ready, shall we make a move?' Gareth interrupted, pushing back his chair, relieving the tense moment, much to Melissa's relief.

'Still feeling lucky?' Melissa asked Peter as they arrived at the brightly lit casino and Blue Moon Club.

'Who wouldn't be, with a girl like you beside me?'

Melissa laughed lightly. 'You're going to hate me if you lose a fortune tonight. Rabbits' feet aren't always to be trusted.'

Peter gave her hand a quick squeeze before returning his own large hand to the steering-wheel. 'You are... I've got a sixth sense.'

Melissa couldn't be sure, but she felt the drop in temperature behind her. She glowed inside with a fickle satisfaction. Now it was her turn to give Gareth something to think about ... if he had the capacity to think about anything else other than the beautiful Dian beside him!

In the casino Peter's intuition proved right. His luck, in the form of Melissa's laughing company and several lucky guesses at the roulette table, prompted him to sweep her into his arms and tell her – and the assembled company – that she was the most wonderful girl in the world.

'I'm not usually a gambling man,' he whispered into her ear, kissing the soft skin of her neck, 'but I'm sorely tempted to change my ways after tonight's good fortune. Just so long as I have you with me, though...'

As Melissa giggled her way out of the strong embrace she noticed to her dismay that both Gareth and Dian were absent, making triumph in Peter's arms seem sadly shortlived.

'They've gone through to the club, I should imagine,' said Peter, following her gaze. 'Suppose we leave them to their own devices and concentrate our energies on the blackjack table?'

Melissa cast her eyes over the burly Australian. 'Perhaps we'd better stop while we're on a winning streak – you wouldn't mind, would you?' Convincing herself she was being sensible, Melissa fought hard to forget the fact that she was dying of curiosity to see what Dian and Gareth were up to.

Peter ran his fingers lightly through her

hair. 'I've only one thing on my mind tonight: the beautiful girl I see before me.'

'Dian's right,' Melissa laughed sweetly, 'you are an idiot – a charming one!'

Relieved that Peter was so easy to handle, Melissa allowed him to sweep her on to the floor of the Blue Moon Club. Through the tangle of dancers she could just make out Dian and Gareth, their bodies glued together, Dian's arms linked snakelike around Gareth's neck. Melissa gulped back her shock as she saw Dian's fingers rove Gareth's hair and fall seductively to the broad shoulders beneath.

'Don't worry about those two,' Peter whispered as he folded her into him, forcing back her attention. 'Dian's a wild one, she can take care of herself. She's not soft and sweet like you…'

He drew his large hand over her back, clasping her so tightly that her breasts were forced into the rough Australian chest, making her jump with surprise. For the first time that evening she felt a pang of anxiety in his company. It was true she was flirting with him a little, but did it matter? Gareth and the vivacious, desirable Dian were enjoying themselves well enough!

'Hey, are you still with me?' Peter's hand slipped to the base of her spine and over the high round cheek of her buttock.

'Peter!' gasped Melissa, wriggling.

'Sorry...' He removed his hand to safer territory. 'As I said, I couldn't resist you...'

'Would a long glass of something cool and refreshing help to quench your ... thirst?' asked Melissa, smiling forgivingly at her partner.

'Maybe.' Giving her a few moments of concern, the muscular arms still refused to let her go. Melissa looked helplessly over the broad shoulder, catching the very last pair of eyes she wanted to see. A look of 'I told you so' flickered across Gareth's face, his lips tensing into a cynical smile.

'Come on, my sweet little Melissa,' whispered Peter, finally giving up the battle to win her attention, and, taking her by the hand, he pulled her through the crowd, relieving her, thank goodness, of the problem of brazening it out in front of Gareth.

'Orange juice and lemonade,' Melissa whispered breathlessly, happy to have got out of a narrow squeak. But by the time Peter had brought drinks she had indulged herself into a quiet anger as she gazed unobserved at every sensual movement Dian was making in Gareth's embrace.

'Having fun?' asked Peter, sliding an arm around her shoulders. 'Or do I get the impression you're mad at me, just a little bit?'

'Oh, Peter,' Melissa gasped, at once contrite, 'of course I'm not mad at you! It's just that...'

'You're worried I'm going to – how do you Brits put it … take advantage?'

Melissa looked sheepishly at him, trying to rid herself of the memory of Gareth's warning and the feeling that she might just have taken on more than she could handle. 'I suppose so. I don't want to be a crashing bore, but I'd hate you to think I was deliberately … leading you on.'

Peter's easy grin widened. 'Listen, you're out with me this evening to enjoy yourself. There's no law that I can't try my luck, is there? On the other hand, I can see the writing on the wall plain enough … you're not that sort of girl … am I right?'

Melissa couldn't help a little giggle at Peter's frankness. Gareth had been absolutely right when he said Australians spoke their minds, and now she was very thankful for it, since she felt she could speak hers too. 'That's not to say I don't find you devastatingly attractive – I do!' she added, glimpsing his expression.

'Well, we can work on it, then,' chuckled Peter, relaxing her into the crook of his arm. 'But, for now, you've got my promise I'll behave.'

'I suppose you've known Gareth a long time,' Melissa asked, changing the subject deliberately, but still feeling Peter's fingers casually stroking the bare skin of her arms.

'I've only met him a couple of times.' Peter

took a healthy gulp of his non-alcoholic lager and fixed her with his blue eyes. 'Sydney's not my territory. My company send me thousands of miles in one month alone... Australia's a big place, you know.'

'So you don't bump into him much?'

'Not much,' he answered stiffly, frowning. 'Hey, what is this? You got something going for the guy ... or am I way off beam?'

Melissa determinedly shook her head. 'That's ridiculous – of course I haven't! Look, you can see those two are...'

'I can see Dian is enjoying herself! But then she always does. No matter how many men she's with – or how few.'

Melissa regarded Peter with a faint curiosity as he watched the octopus-like movements of his sister.

'Come on, let's have some fun and break them up,' he said with a devilish glint in his blue eyes. 'If I can make Dian mad enough, we'll see fireworks free of charge!' He pulled Melissa on to the floor and she found herself standing in bewilderment as he tapped Gareth lightly on the shoulder. 'Mind if we break up the party?'

Surprisingly the dark-eyed creature sank into her brother's arms without demur, and when Gareth swept Melissa into his she could hardly believe the touch of the teasing lips kissing her lightly as though he barely noticed the change-over!

'Wh-what did you do that for?' stammered Melissa, stunned by the quick-fire warmth of his lips on hers. Not wanting him to think she had been craving his attention all evening, she gave a careless shrug of her slim shoulders. As he brought her firmly to him, his fingertips sending shivers of delight along her spine, her body responded eagerly, betraying her true desires with a force that made her gasp. If only it could have been like this with Peter! If only she had felt an iota of what she was feeling now, dizzy with delight, desperately overwhelmed and totally vulnerable in the presence of the sensual body pressing against her.

'I kissed you because I felt like it,' he growled challengingly, nuzzling her ear, making her heart soar with a wonderful, illogical excitement. 'Besides which, you've given our Australian friend every opportunity to paw you! Now it's my turn.'

Melissa jerked away from him, angry pink dots inflaming her cheeks. 'Peter was not pawing me!'

'What the hell was he doing, then? What polite name would you give it?' grated Gareth, keeping a firm hold on her.

The blood boiled in her veins as she narrowed her eyes at him. 'I'd call it no more than having fun, the same kind of fun you were having with Dian … or have you any objection to a woman enjoying herself to the same degree as a man?'

'No, only women who take it to the limit, who flirt outrageously and lead a man into believing she's game for casual sex.'

Melissa stopped still on the dance-floor, not caring now who saw or overheard her. Trembling from head to foot, she retaliated in tones which left him in no doubt as to her finer feelings. 'I don't know why you dislike me so much, Gareth, and frankly, I don't care! But I don't have to stand here listening to the rubbish you talk. Please let go of me. I don't want to dance with you. I don't want to even have to look at you!'

How stupid, how gullible she had been! Here was the stereotype woman-chaser who, at the root of things, was paradoxically jealous of another man's capability to impress a woman. What had she seen in him? What single reason could she give herself to explain the insanity of falling under the spell of a bigoted, conceited, arrogant fool like Gareth Tremaine?

Suddenly the music softened, slipping from the upbeat tempo of a popular melody to the slow, rhythmic harmony of a love song. Predictably she felt the hesitation in Gareth's grip and a slight relaxation of the fingers clasping her. She prepared herself to be abandoned. Instead, Gareth pulled her closer, running his arm more tightly around her waist, a movement which held her spellbound as the physical desire for him which she thought had drowned over the last few seconds was resurrected again, filling her with indescribable relief, then a mounting, utterly incomprehensible pleasure.

'Peter's crazy about you – you do know that, I suppose?' The deep, slightly faltering voice sounded at her ear, his cheek pressed against her hair as they moved, unaware of the other dancers.

'That's ... not true,' stammered Melissa, unable to move an inch in his arms – not that she could if she wanted to! The warm, sensual touch of his fingers caressed her back.

'You'll find out ... but don't say I haven't warned you.'

She could hardly speak, she didn't care about Peter – at least, not in that sense, and she had given him no cause to think she did. What she did care about was the man who held her so tenderly in his arms, the man who could turn her wintry feelings into a breath of beautiful summer simply by the sound of his voice.

'Lost your tongue?' Gareth whispered lazily through her hair, his body filling her with the most unutterable delight as he swayed in step, holding her so tightly. 'I thought all women were moved to a response when it came to the subject of love.'

'We aren't talking about love,' Melissa croaked, feeling the fingers curl at her neck and entwine gently in her hair. 'Peter's not in love – at least, not with me. We haven't known each other five minutes.'

'Don't you believe in love at first sight?'

Melissa checked her own hesitant breath, staring up into the glimmering eyes which roved her face, capturing her heart and mind and senses for all her trying to be free. 'I've never been asked that before. I don't know if I can give you an answer.'

'Try. It's not such a difficult question, is it?'

It was a question Melissa was to ponder for many hours ahead, and one she was excused the problem of answering by the timely interruption of Dian, who had tired of her brother's company.

'Do you mind if we go now, Gareth?' the dark beauty asked with acid sweetness, arriving at Gareth's side. 'It's getting rather crowded in here, and I must admit to having the smallest of headaches.'

On the journey homeward Melissa wondered just what had happened to her this evening. It seemed like a dream, too far-fetched to be real. The one whose face she longed to look at sat directly behind her, obscured from her view even if she managed to look out of the corner of her eyes.

In all her life, Melissa had never been able to convince herself that anything worthwhile was not obtained without a great deal of hard work. Love, she had decided, was no exception. And she had imagined that the mystical, magical presence in her life which she would one day call love would come after a great deal of sensible reasoning over the right partner. Love was eternal. So how, in a split-second, could any human being know true love?

Melissa wondered if Gareth was holding Dian in the back seat. She could hear nothing, sense nothing. She would, at this moment, give a great deal to have eyes in the back of her head!

CHAPTER EIGHT

'Sleep well,' Gareth murmured as Melissa closed her door that night.

And, almost as if it were the most natural thing in the world, he had kissed her, his lips warmly persuasive on hers. But he'd made no move to follow her into her room – and with Dian pleading for an aspirin down-stairs Melissa guessed she was safe!

The next few days flew by, making her wonder if the Blue Moon Club had ever happened. Surgery had never been so busy, minor ops taking precedence over the open clinics, so that very often when she and

Gareth finished their work late in the evenings she felt too tired to parry his occasional barbed cynicisms about Peter hanging around the house waiting for her appearance. The fact that Dian was prowling the rooms like a caged tigress seemed to have slipped his notice completely!

Now, on Wednesday morning during a quiet spell, Walter Forbes sat in the office checking the beagle's blood results. 'Gareth diagnoses pulmonic stenosis, I see...' The locum vet watched Melissa through large spectacles balancing precariously on an old, weather-beaten nose.

'Yes, that's right. Dan's been in for observation for five days now, and Gareth suspects that the symptoms are right-sided congestive failure,' Melissa added, casting her mind back to her last conversation with Gareth at nine-thirty this morning before he'd gone out to the Langtons' farm on an emergency call.

Walter Forbes grunted his approval. At sixty-three he was still an efficient vet, but Melissa knew he would not be too keen to undertake surgery in Gordon's absence. Now he was in semi-retirement, his hearth and slippers took priority rather than the up-to-date techniques of operating theatres.

'Surgically enlarging the defect is possible,' Walter agreed, lighting up his pipe as he leaned back in his chair. 'I never used these newfangled methods myself. Gareth going to undertake the job?'

'Only if you agree with the diagnosis – and don't want to do the op yourself,' Melissa added kindly.

Walter grinned, folding his arms across an ample girth. 'I think I'll pass on this one. I'm quite happy to leave all the hard work to the young 'uns these days. Still, Gareth's a good lad to offer me first refusal. He always was a considerate youngster, even in his teens.'

'You've known him a long time?' asked Melissa, suddenly curious.

'Certainly have. Had hopes he'd be my son-in-law one day. But my Lissa didn't know when she was on to a good thing – left him to go and "find herself" in one of those commune places, all beads and chanting, that sort of stuff. Didn't last long, I'm happy to say.'

Melissa thought Walter's Lissa had probably had a lucky escape. Beads and chanting were a lot less harmless than Gareth's cunning brand of charisma!

'Off Gareth went, bold as brass, to Australia ... intent on making good,' rejoined Walter sympathetically. 'Lots of ambition, that boy. Good to see him back home now. Though I think if it hadn't been for Gordon's troubles we might have lost a damn good chap. Too many of our young fellas being enticed abroad.'

Gareth's ambition had hardly got him very far, Melissa thought bitterly. In the end he had come back to England where he knew a nest egg would be waiting to fall into his hands!

She swung round to see the Land Rover jerk to a halt in the car park, becoming uncomfortably aware of a phenomenon that was fast becoming the norm in her life – a distinct increase in the rate of her heartbeat! Why, she asked herself for the umpteenth time, her colour rising, when she knew what kind of character Gareth really was, did she behave in this ridiculous childish way?

Gareth walked into the office seconds later, shirt-sleeves still rolled up from his tussle with a Friesian cow, his muscular brown forearms displaying the first hint of English sun.

'Langton's cow responded,' he proclaimed triumphantly, 'and the rest of the herd are clear of trouble. The intra-mammary antibiotic will do the job quickly enough once the sub-clinical bacterial infection is killed... Melissa?'

Melissa realised she had been staring at him idiotically and had not heard a word. She bit her bottom lip as a fresh flood of colour rushed to her face. 'What? Oh, sorry, my mind was elsewhere.'

'And I wonder where...' Gareth raised an

eyebrow in her direction. She could have sworn a smile flickered across his lips at the sight of her obvious embarrassment!

'I'll just check on Mrs Carter–' she muttered, flustered.

'Before you rush off...' Gareth caught her by the arm. 'I'm going out to the Oldfields Estate this afternoon. Like to come with me? I've got rather a large dog with possible hind limb ataxia. The call came in just before I left for Langton's this morning.'

Melissa stood uncertainly, trying to ignore the feeling of sudden light-headedness. She was stunned by Gareth's offer, and no less stunned by the tingling sensation of her skin beneath his fingertips.

'You heard about Oldfields, did you?' Walter poked his head through the pipe fog. 'They're demolishing it. I'd be careful if I were you – there are reported cases of muggings in the newspapers.'

Gareth shrugged his large shoulders. 'Can't be helped – there's no way they can bring the dog in.'

Melissa suddenly woke up from her reverie, realising just how much the suggestion of fieldwork appealed to her, even if it was in Gareth's company. They had been working so hard recently that a run through the Dorset countryside would be heavenly at this time of the year.

'Walter, you don't mind staying for

surgery this afternoon?' asked Gareth.

'Not at all, old boy. Grace knows where I am. Tomorrow, though, I'm being dragged into Dorlington for a shopping spree, so I won't be in again until Friday. Do you know when your father's coming back?'

Gareth shook his head, his attention taken by a car arriving outside. 'Not heard a word yet – ah, this looks like the beagle's owners. Would you like to see them with me, Walter? I'd value a second opinion.'

'Nothing I could add to your diagnosis, lad,' Walter said gratefully, knocking out his pipe on the waste-paper basket. 'My days of specialised surgery are over – and all the pressure that goes with them, thank God.'

Melissa watched Gareth disappear into his treatment-room, thinking just how tactful he could be when he wanted. It was a pity he didn't show more consideration to the women in his life!

Mrs Carter rang through from the kitchen to say lunch was ready, and with an unusually light heart Melissa informed Walter of the delicious menu. It had been odd in the house without the Tremaines ... now perhaps, with Mrs Carter's culinary skills, the place would resume its normal homely atmosphere.

Melissa's light heart lasted as long as the first course.

Mrs Carter positioned her next to Gareth – purposely, Melissa decided, as reprisal against Dian for the fruit cake! Dian, seated between her brother and the chatty Walter, was treated to a dissertation on the ups and downs of growing monster marrows.

'I'm afraid the Grays have decided against further treatment on Dan,' Gareth told Melissa as he came in. 'As he's nearly nine, they feel surgery will be too much for him.'

Melissa gazed into Mrs Carter's home-made tomato soup and hoped her cheeks weren't reflecting its hue, for she could feel Dian's gaze freezing the spoon in her hand. 'Do you think he stands a chance?' she asked quietly.

Gareth shook his head as he began his meal. 'The right ventricle is having to work much harder to pump blood into the lungs. It might fail. On the other hand...'

'Do the Grays know?'

'I've explained the condition generally, but Dan has his good phases and I think they're hoping he'll recover. Turning a blind eye, I suppose. Natural enough.'

Mrs Carter wafted away the soup plates and produced a mouthwatering quiche and hot new potatoes. 'Delicious, Mrs Carter!' Gareth enthused, trying to dodge the arrowed gaze of Dian.

'It's a narrowing of the pulmonary artery, isn't it?' Walter enquired, directing a laden fork into his mouth, forgetting momentarily his marrows.

'Exactly. Diet and exercise aren't going to cure it. Surgery is inevitable.'

'Thank goodness there is something you can do,' Melissa murmured gratefully.

'We've two options surgically,' Gareth began, his intense green eyes causing her skin to flutter under the enthusiasm of his words. 'The first is–'

'Doesn't anyone *ever* talk about something other than animals in this house?' Dian suddenly cut in, relegating her knife and fork noisily to her untouched plate. 'That's all I've heard for the past few days – animals, operations, running tests, left and right ven … whatever you call them! There are other things in life, you know, Gareth!'

Gareth smiled calmly. 'Such as?'

Dian stared petulantly across the table, tendrils of black hair trembling with emotion as she spoke. 'Such as you and me, of course! When are we going to have time to ourselves, Gareth?'

Melissa waited with bated breath, uncomfortably aware that everyone had stopped eating.

It was Peter who broke the silence, laughing self-consciously as though his sister had made some kind of joke. 'You'll have to excuse Dian, she's not one to sit and twiddle her thumbs – or listen politely to conversation that frankly bores her.'

'Shut up, Peter!' Dian turned contemptuously on her brother, her lovely face contorting with suppressed anger. 'I don't need you to speak for me. If this is the only way I'm going to get your attention, Gareth, then so be it. The others will just have to put up with it. I want a few answers and I want them now!'

'Any time,' Gareth murmured silkily.

The dark-eyed girl fixed her icy gaze on Melissa. 'I want to know what's going on between you two. I didn't come all this way to be fobbed off with a silly story about her simply being your father's assistant. I believe you and she were ... involved ... before you came to Australia. I think you've been writing silly letters to one another – and don't bother denying it, either of you!'

Melissa couldn't believe what she was hearing. So this was why Dian disliked her so much! She really believed that she and Gareth had had an affair ... and naturally Gareth's teasing behaviour at the Blue Moon had only served to compound her suspicions.

'I read the letters you sent him!' blurted Dian, colour rising to her cheeks. 'I found them in a drawer beside his bed and I read them – all of them. You poor little thing, believing he'd come back to you. Did you think he would? Did you think he'd leave me for someone like you?'

At this remark Melissa's mounting fury burst the banks of good sense. As she jumped to her feet she remembered vaguely registering Mrs Carter's look of astonishment and Walter spluttering into his coffee.

'I don't give a damn whose letters you found!' she hissed between gritted teeth. 'They certainly weren't mine! But let me tell you here and now, if I wanted to impress Gareth by flitting around like a psychedelic butterfly I've no doubt I could do it. But as it happens, medical techniques appeal to me much more ... and if Gareth wants to talk about them for the next decade I shall be quite content to sit and listen to him!'

Dian's bottom lip quivered under the careful application of plum-pink lip-gloss. The Australian girl fled the table so quickly she nearly knocked Mrs Carter flying.

Peter got up quickly to follow her. 'Look, I'm sorry, everyone... Gareth, you know how she can be at times...'

'I know, Peter,' Gareth muttered darkly. 'You'd better go. When she's cooled down I'll come and talk to her.'

Peter disappeared from the kitchen, his square shoulders rounded dejectedly, fleetingly glancing an apology in Melissa's direction.

'My, my!' mumbled Walter, patting his midriff and eyeing Mrs Carter's untouched profiteroles. 'It must have been my marrows

175

that sparked off the temper tantrum. Grace is inclined to go a bit red in the face when I go overboard about them.'

''Twasn't your marrows, Mr Forbes,' retorted Mrs Carter meaningfully, lowering a plate of succulent profiteroles and a jug of cream on to the table.

Still shaking, Melissa stared unseeing at the chocolate-covered delicacies with their creamy filling. She was trying to think of what she had said, and she had the horrible feeling that in order to spite Dian she had paid Gareth the most unwarranted compliment – and in front of the whole household too!

Suddenly a large arm swept around her shoulders. 'I had no idea how much I'd impressed you, Melissa my sweet! So I'm assured of your loyal attentions for the next ten years!' Then with a look that made her seethe with indignation he added, 'I shall of course kept you to your word.'

Number seventy-one Marsh Road looked as deserted as the other downtrodden houses of the Oldfields Estate. To the north, new buildings in red brick had been erected with tall wooden fences to separate them from the crumbling eyesore of the old complex.

Gareth pulled on the handbrake and turned to slide an arm behind Melissa. 'Feeling better, or do I detect a definite change to sub-zero temperatures?'

Melissa longed to repudiate her mood, since she had kept silent throughout the journey other than to give directions. But she was still angry, and if she admitted the truth to herself her temper had got to boiling point when she saw Dian's head buried in Gareth's chest just before leaving.

'I didn't hear you telling her she was wrong about us,' she snapped, unable to dismiss the picture of Gareth's arms supporting a sobbing Dian.

'Oh, she wouldn't have listened ... you know what Dian is.'

Melissa turned impatiently in her seat, glaring at the arm still lazing behind her, 'I'm fed up with everyone making excuses for her! You gave me no support at all. It's as if you wanted her to think you and I are having ... having–'

'An affair, I think the expression is,' Gareth drawled sardonically.

'So you did try to make her jealous! You used me as bait and I just happened to fall into your trap!'

'I didn't force you to say all those nice things...'

'Huh! I just don't understand you, Gareth!'

'The eternal cry of most women, my darling – I am allowed to call you that now, aren't I? After all, you did say you were prepared to hang on my every word for the–'

'I am not your darling, and you can forget what I said in front of Dian,' snapped Melissa.

'Ah, so the truth will out! You accuse me of titillating Dian, and yet you tell a whopper like that, cravenly exciting me and sending Dian into fits of tears.'

Melissa stared at him with her large grey eyes already narrowing dangerously into devilish slits. 'Gareth! You are the most smooth-talking, infuriating–'

'All right, all right, I get your point.' Gareth ducked in mock fear as he withdrew his arm and sat looking the picture of innocence.

Melissa shut her open mouth – with an effort. She thought irritably of the journey she had intended to enjoy and how it had all been soured by lunchtime's events. Mostly she was hurt. Hurt because Dian had been the one to end up in Gareth's arms and Dian was the one who had started the whole stupid thing in the first place!

'This is it?' Gareth squinted disbelievingly at the overgrown grass someone once must have used as a lawn. 'You're sure we're at the right place?'

'According to the directions you gave me,' Melissa answered coolly, trying to force her mind back to the object of their visit.

'It looks empty. There's even chipboard

nailed over the lower window. Wait … there's someone waving us in. Come on!'

Melissa trailed Gareth to the house, surveying the broad shoulders and curling dark hair and trying to tell herself she had decided in the last five minutes on the answer of falling in love at first sight. It had to be an impossibility! If ever she were to fall in love it would be with someone who had the courage to stand by her through thick and thin – and someone who didn't have a squad of girlfriends popping into his life every five minutes!

'Mrs Giles? I'm Gareth Tremaine. I spoke to you earlier today.'

A small, unkempt-looking woman peered distrustfully up at them, muttering under her breath. Melissa quickly forgot her annoyance with Gareth as she kept close to his reassuring figure on the journey down a gloomy, dank-smelling hallway.

'We're being moved out tomorrow,' Mrs Giles told them brusquely, leading the way into a shabby room where a youth lay straddled across a chair, his huge boots digging into what was left of the upholstery.

The surly face continued with its observance of the blaring television, ignoring Gareth's polite, 'Good afternoon.'

'Bruce is out here.' The woman led the way through a grimy, paint-peeling kitchen. 'He keeps having accidents, so we put him in the outhouse.'

As she opened the door of the shed they were met by the sorry gaze of a large black dog lying on a blanket cushioned by newspapers.

'How long has he been in this condition?' asked Gareth abruptly, bending down to examine the dog.

'A couple of days, I suppose it must be. But he's been bad on his back legs for a long while. He's all of thirteen now.' Mrs Giles turned to Melissa and sighed. 'We haven't had much luck in this family. The boy's father died, I've been ill, Kevin's out of work. And now the dog–'

Fortuitously for Melissa a call from the house took her scurrying indoors.

'I'm afraid it's not good,' muttered Gareth as Melissa knelt down beside him and drew her fingers over the scruffy animal coat. How small all her troubles seemed when faced with circumstances like these.

'It's a chronic degenerative condition,' Gareth told her as he examined the paralysed limbs. 'German Shepherds are often prone to it, though any larger dog is susceptible. His back paws have been knuckling – you can see how the nails are scored.' He gently lifted a back leg for Melissa to examine. 'The central nervous system is affected. We might have been able to give him some treatment before this final attack,

180

but as you can see, he's now paraplegic.'

'You mean we can't do anything for him … take him back to the surgery? Surely we can…?'

Gareth shook his head, deep lines of concern contorting his face. Melissa felt an overwhelming sadness as he laid a comforting arm around her shoulders. 'It's best he doesn't suffer any more, you know that as well as I do.'

Mrs Giles returned, and Gareth broke the news to her.

'I thought as much,' she said bravely. 'You'd better get on with it. I'll be in the house.'

Soon the dog entered his last sleep, peaceful and pain-free.

'Are you all right?' Gareth asked Melissa gently.

She nodded, feeling her eyes mist. He suddenly caught her glance and she knew that whatever their personal differences, the grief and sense of loss they shared over extinguishing a life was mutual. She had watched his tenderness with the animal and saw the concern in his deep-set eyes … when he reached across and held her hand she simply clung to the reassuring fingers. Perhaps it was then she realised she was losing the battle to keep him out of her heart, and no matter what she told herself about his self-centred approach to life or his cavalier attitude towards women, nothing could change the powerful magnetism drawing her irrevocably towards him.

She gulped back her emotion and drew away her hand as Mrs Giles reappeared with her son.

'Leave him with us,' Mrs Giles told them. 'We'll all be gone from here tomorrow. Bruce can stay where he's lived all his life.'

'Are you sure?' asked Gareth, concerned.

'Kevin and me will do what's needed.' And, indicating that they should follow her, she led them back through the house. 'I can't afford to pay you very much...'

'Leave the account until a more convenient time,' said Gareth quietly. 'I'm very sorry about Bruce.'

Back in the Land Rover Melissa found herself too miserable to talk.

'Are you OK?' Gareth asked as he leaned to switch on the engine.

Glancing out of the window at the concrete pillars in the distance, Melissa nodded. The graveyard of houses beneath the spiralling futuristic road made her shudder.

'Come on, cheer up,' he urged her, engaging first gear and driving on to the road. 'Try to remember you can't sort out everyone's problems, you just have to do what you can – even if it's only a little bit.'

Melissa smiled at him, knowing the logic

of what he was saying, but, watching the road uninterestedly, she hardly noticed him stop the vehicle in a deserted lay-by. 'Damn place is like a ghost town!' he cursed. 'Let's have a look at those directions again.'

Melissa opened the briefly sketched map on her knees.

'We should be about here,' mused Gareth, tracing Marsh Road with his finger. Melissa listened to the deep voice, her eyes lingering foolishly over the dark lashes fanning the cheeks. Her heart ached when she saw ragged furrows of tension creeping across his brow, and she had to physically stop herself from wrapping her arms round him and running her fingertips over the roughness of his beard, which seemed so attractively evident at this moment.

'This is where we've gone wrong,' Gareth told her, unaware, luckily, of her restless yearnings inside. 'We shall have to turn round, take the third on our left–'

A noise outside made him stop in mid-sentence.

Melissa looked up, startled. To her horror a man's face glared menacingly in at the window, and before she knew what was happening she felt Gareth pull her roughly to him, at the same time slamming his hand on the lock of her door.

'Trouble!' he muttered as the man moved to the bonnet. 'I think we'd better get out of here.' He reached for the starter. But almost before the words had been spoken his door flew open.

'Get out!' commanded another dirty, unshaven youth. 'And the girl too!'

'The keys are in the ignition; if you see me having trouble, drive off – with your foot hard down,' Gareth whispered hurriedly. And in an instant he had sprung out of the Land Rover, slamming the door firmly behind him.

Melissa stared in horror as he stood talking to the two men. She tried to listen to what was being said, but she could only hear the erratic pounding of her own heartbeat. Almost jumping out of her seat when the younger man aggressively pushed Gareth's shoulder, she forced herself to sit still.

To her astonishment Gareth took the blow as though it had hardly touched him, his hands casually out of sight in his pockets, the only clue to his true feelings a small muscle jerking at the base of his jaw.

Melissa closed her eyes, feeling a cold sweat break over her body. Should she consider leaving Gareth to defend himself if a fight started? It would be simple enough to slip over to the driver's seat, lock the door and flick on the ignition and perhaps try to reach help? But she knew it was not an option she could even consider. Please God, he would be safe ... please God! was all she could hope and pray.

Suddenly the sound of the driver's door echoed in her ears. Her whole body stiffened as she thought of what might be about to happen to her.

'Don't say a word...'

Melissa opened her eyes to see Gareth sitting in the driver's seat, his face very pale. She felt the engine roar into life as the vehicle swerved around into the direction from which they had come towards the lights of the motorway.

'Thank heavens!' sighed Melissa, letting out her breath and cupping her face in her hands. 'They let you go...'

'You should have done as I told you, Melissa, and got the hell out of it!' he almost shouted at her. 'Did you think I was joking?'

She swallowed, her throat dry and her legs feeling like jelly. 'It all happened so quickly ... but I'd never have left you with those thugs, no matter what you told me!'

He provided her with a spectacular grin. 'You were spitting nails at me earlier – now you're saying you'd never leave me!'

'It was just... I couldn't let you face them alone!'

'That's exactly what I was worried about,' Gareth returned sharply. 'How do you think I'd have felt if you'd been hurt or they'd carted you off somewhere?'

'At this moment in time – pleased to be

rid of me with a valid excuse!' Melissa observed with a wry smile, silently picturing Dian's delight at the news of her unfortunate dispatch.

'Probably,' Gareth confirmed lightly, then, touching her arm with reassuring fingers, he added, 'You're sure you're all right?'

'I ... I think so. What was it all about?'

'Apparently there were scuffles on the estate. They thought we were spies for the officials trying to relocate them. The area has long been condemned, you see. I had to convince them that I was simply a vet.'

'They must have believed you!'

'I told them Mrs Giles could vouch for us. That seemed to allay their fears, although I rather think the younger chap wasn't too sure.'

'I don't think I've ever been quite so frightened,' murmured Melissa, hardly realising she was cuddling up to Gareth for his body warmth. A strange feeling was overtaking her, a delicious lassitude which her practical mind conveniently explained as shock.

'Comfortable?' he asked in a voice that seemed to come from just by her ear.

'Mmm...' She allowed her heavy lids to flutter downwards, savouring the steady drone of the engine, Gareth's body supporting her own ... she was too tired to think any more ... too tired. Try as she might, she couldn't disentangle herself from the arm and shoulder she was nuzzling. The smell of his aftershave, so earthily sensual, though exciting her, was also ferrying her into a sleepy, breathtaking vortex where dreams were already beginning to form...

She woke in darkness, knowing that something had changed in her life. Changed sufficiently enough for her to be resting in the arms of a man, his soft breath on her cheek.

'It's all right ... take your time ... don't panic.' Gareth's voice came lazily through lips just a fraction away from her upturned head. 'You fell asleep and I didn't have the heart to wake you.'

Melissa tried to move and felt his arms encircle her protectively and firmly. 'Just wake up slowly. You had a nasty shock; your pulse was rather rapid earlier.'

'You ... you took it?' Melissa gasped, her hand involuntarily running over her hot body. What else, she wondered, had he checked while she was asleep?

As usual, reading her thoughts, he did nothing to put her mind at rest. 'This is the most unresisting I've found you, here in my arms sleeping like a baby.'

'I feel fine now,' she lied, trying to ease herself upwards, terrified he might try to kiss her because, if he did, at this moment she would have no strength to resist him.

Her own lack of sexual experience was proving a terrible disadvantage, in the face of his undoubted skill. Did he know her inner components seemed to be having a frenzied game of squash inside her – with her heart as the ball?

She blinked at the mirage of his face and for the first time wondered where she was.

'Are we home?' she asked croakily, the veil of sleep slipping from her mind and exposing the true reality, Gareth's arms tightly around her, his eyes like fiery gemstones set in the craggy darkness of his face.

'Yes, unfortunately! I was just beginning to enjoy myself.'

'Gareth!' Her trembling voice reflected her nervous struggle to sit upright, the absurd thought possessing her that she had been unable to prevent any advances he had made while she'd slept so soundly.

'With a woman in his arms and the moon up there smiling down – and no one to see, no man couldn't be blamed for enjoying himself ... just a little!'

'Gareth, you haven't...!' Melissa attacked the buttons of her dress and the soft delicate material draping her knees. All was intact – she hoped!

'You'll never know, will you?' he said teasingly, unwrapping her, and, reaching across to unlock her door, he gave her one last heart-jerking moment as his body lingered heavily over hers. 'Don't want to set the tongues wagging, do we?' he whispered before he pulled away from her, easing her steadily by the waist and allowing her to slip from the vehicle.

Melissa stood in a state of disorientation. The night was as soft as a rose petal. The aroma of freshly cut grass lingered in the air. Tall pines oozed spring sap from deep, rough crevices in their bark and the moon was a full silver saucer that lingered overhead, spreading its light as generously as its magic.

When Gareth slipped an arm round her in order to guide her to the house she wondered when she would really wake up. For this, surely, must still be a dream?

CHAPTER NINE

Melissa surveyed the shepherd's pie steaming on the plate before her. Expert patterns wove their way across its crust and thick gravy dribbled over the spring greens. But she found she could hardly eat a scrap. Perhaps coming home to spend a few hours with Gramps and Eileen hadn't been such a good idea after all!

'That's not like you,' grumbled her grandfather. 'You've got an appetite like a horse as a rule. What's happened? Have you two been at one another's throats again?'

Eileen Purdy and Augustus Moon exchanged meaningful glances across the dining table. 'You go and sit down, Gusty, and I'll see to the washing-up,' Eileen said gently.

'I'll help you,' offered Melissa, gathering the plates.

She began the washing-up in the kitchen, and soon the day's events had been related over the soapsuds, Eileen Purdy listening attentively and Melissa pouring out her story. She hesitated at the part where she had fallen asleep to wake in Gareth's arms ... it didn't seem very believable put into words!

Eileen put the last dish in the cupboard, her eyes twinkling. 'It took a lot of bravery to stand up to those men,' she said, taking a long look at Melissa. 'And by the sound of it he was very cross that you didn't make an escape.'

Melissa nodded, sinking on to a stool.

'Which can only make me think he has your interests at heart, dear.'

'And the interests of the whole female population in general, I imagine,' Melissa stressed, brushing back the cloud of fair hair from her face.

'You know,' Eileen said slowly, putting the kettle on to boil, 'this Dian person doesn't sound like Gareth's type at all. Have you thought she could be making a mountain out of a molehill? Perhaps Gareth's involvement with her isn't what you think it is.'

'Even if it isn't,' Melissa said doubtfully, 'what about the other girl, the one whose letters he keeps by his bed – and for all I know dozens of others who've passed through his life on a conveyor belt?'

Eileen gave a faint chuckle, looking at the young woman whose pretty face was shadowed with uncertainty. 'Come now, Melissa, Gareth is a kind man. He doesn't try to extort money from his clients, nor does he seem to me to be the type of person who'd run away from his responsibilities. Do you really think you have the full story? Wouldn't it be a good idea to ask Gareth himself?'

Melissa sighed, smiling wistfully. 'What would I say to him, Eileen? "Have you really come back to England just to cash in on your father's money? Is it true you ran out on Dian, and just what are your feelings for her now?" Oh, he'd probably just laugh at me – he enjoys seeing me struggling like a schoolgirl trying to find something constructive to say in his presence!'

Eileen squeezed the small hand. 'Gareth's an older man; he's probably known a lot of sophisticated women–'

'Which makes me feel all the more inadequate!'

Eileen shook her grey head fiercely. 'You didn't feel like that when you first met him, when you mistook him for a complete stranger, did you? From what you tell me you acted with a great deal of confidence … right up until the time Dian arrived on the scene.'

Melissa felt a terrible physical ache when she thought of the moment she had first met Dian. Every instinct in her body had cried out for it not to be true, although at the time she wouldn't admit that reaction to herself. 'Maybe you're right. But surely it's impossible to feel the way I do about him!'

Eileen smiled. 'All I can say is, if you love the man – and don't let's mince words, the word is love for a girl like you – then don't let anyone or anything come in your way. Until he tells you himself that he doesn't want you, don't give up. Don't ever give up!'

Eileen Purdy's words lingered in Melissa's mind as she returned to the surgery late that evening, locking the Mini and walking across to the darkened house. Love was madness … it had to be. Who in their right mind would fall for someone so obviously unsuited for the role of husband, lover – faithful lover! – and loyal, lifelong companion? But no matter how she reasoned it, her body over which she was having less and less control lately yearned for him – and even when he wasn't here, her thoughts were always driven to him, the newly awakened urges within her making nonsense of all her practical, sensible plans for the future.

Melissa steeled herself, realising she had to run the gauntlet of getting to her bedroom.

She must surely bump into someone – and at this moment she didn't know who she would like to see least. She was tired and ached for bed and the curative blessing of sleep.

Letting herself in by the kitchen door with the key Rose had given her, she tiptoed through the dark kitchen. A warm nose nuzzled into her thigh and she bent down to snuggle up to Susie.

'Everyone gone to bed, darling?' She felt Susie's flat wet nose at her ear as if in answer. 'Has your master walked you?'

The whispered question was, of course, quite unnecessary, for Gareth would have walked Susie and Beetle too, who was now responding well to the bitch's company.

A warm glow filled Melissa as she thought of Eileen Purdy's advice and the possibility of following it … then an equally cold shiver passed through her as she heard Dian's voice in the distance with its high ringing quality.

She jumped up, realising that the household was not asleep – but out! Peter's and Dian's voices mingled, coming from somewhere at the front of the house, possibly the car park.

Gently opening and closing the kitchen door and slipping along the hallway, Melissa took the stairs two at a time, very lightly. At the top of the house, grasping the handle of her bedroom door and turning it very gently so as not to disturb Gareth who had probably crashed out, she began to creep into her room.

Then she heard it. She stopped still, listening.

First a few low tones she recognised with a jerking heart and then louder, swelling with the excited female voice. So Gareth was part of the happy band of warriors! How stupid she was to believe he'd stay in … why should he? Did she think that simply because he had flirted with her it meant anything? Of course it didn't!

She listened with her ear to the door, torturing herself as the distorted sounds rose from the hall beneath. Sounds that made her shudder from head to toe. Gareth could use his charm indiscriminately with any woman he wanted, and, chillingly, Melissa knew she was just another gullible victim.

At last she admitted the awful truth as she crouched listening like a thief in the night – he was the last man in the world she ought to have fallen in love with – a man who loved himself first and the rest of woman-kind next!

She waited to hear his footsteps on the landing, and, changing her mind about locking the door, she slid back the latch, not knowing quite what she was going to do or say – but when she heard him come to his room, however late, she would confront him! Dots of anger and humiliation burned on her cheeks, a speech began in her mind and begged to be released.

She flung herself on the bed with her elbow propping her head – and promptly fell fast asleep.

Rising at six, Melissa felt as though she had a hangover. Her bones ached and her head sang – probably from the Yoga position into which she had curled in the night in order to keep warm.

Showering and breakfasting, she walked Susie to blow away the cobwebs and the non-existent hangover. At least if she had had too much to drink she would have enjoyed herself enough to warrant her feeling like this! She just hoped the three late-night revellers would feel equally jaded this morning.

Pushing open the garden gate, she was to be instantly disappointed as Gareth's sea-green eyes, as fresh and as disconcertingly teasing as usual, welcomed her.

'Morning, Melissa! What unearthly hour did you get up this morning?'

Melissa irritably checked Susie on the lead. 'Sit, Susie! Some of us get our full eight hours' quota of sleep, Gareth – though that might surprise you.'

Annoyingly, Gareth laughed away the insinuation. 'We did make a bit of a racket coming in, I'm afraid ... did you hear us?'

'It didn't bother me at all. I slept like a log.'

Now why did she say that? she asked herself furiously. Where was the carefully compiled speech from last night, the one in which she was going to tell him that at the weekend he could find himself someone else to help him in the surgery, as she was moving back home? She had fulfilled her responsibilities towards Gordon ... if Gareth found himself short-handed no doubt Dian would be the first to offer to mop up a dirty floor, hold down a wriggling patient who attempted to relieve you of your fingers and check throughout the night the temperatures and pulses of any animals who must be observed!

Melissa opened her mouth – and said nothing.

Gareth tilted his dark head to one side, raising a bushy eyebrow, looking almost as though he knew what she was thinking and daring her to ask it.

'Tell you what,' he said with his gaze wandering over her light sweater and jeans, 'since you're dressed for outdoors, come and have a look at Beetle. I think you'll be surprised.'

Melissa, hating herself for following, meekly surveyed the wide shoulders and the large green wellies moving with such magnetic physical grace in front of her. Why couldn't she have the courage of her convictions and say what she felt? Why was she weak as a kitten, as intoxicated in his presence as though she had drunk champagne, and, come to think of it, why had he seemed to cure her hangover when the fresh morning breeze hadn't?

To Melissa's surprise, Beetle ran to greet them as they entered the large grassy compound. But rather than jumping up the dog came immediately to heel at Gareth's commands, playing with Susie when he was bidden.

'Well, what do you think?' he asked, rolling the large Rottweiler on his back and stroking his round barrel chest. A long pink tongue flopped gratefully around the wet jaws.

'You've done wonders, Gareth,' Melissa heard herself saying, and, feeling the powerful animal body wriggle upwards to rub itself lovingly against her knees, she knew it was true.

Gareth did have a magic. A wonderful magic.

He believed in himself, in his power to change, to improve and to heal. And yet, when it came to relationships, these were games to him, cat-and-mouse games! How was it he always found someone to join in the charades with him? How was it that a sensible girl like herself could see right through him and yet be so utterly, helplessly besotted by him?

'Back you go,' Gareth was saying, guiding Beetle back into the run. 'Next walk lunchtime.'

Melissa caught hold of Susie, fixed the lead on her choker chain and began to guide her towards the house.

'Feeling better?' asked Gareth, catching up with her. 'We didn't see you at supper last night, so I guessed you had an early night.'

'I spent the evening with my grandfather and Eileen. I hardly think my company would have been appreciated here,' Melissa averred, pulling Susie on.

Before he had time to answer, Dian's voice echoed from an upstairs window. Looking back over his shoulder, Melissa overheard the muted curse, 'Damn!'

Obviously Gareth was annoyed that Dian had caught them talking together – and alone in the garden too. Well, serve him right! Perhaps there was something she could do ... something to make the situation just a little more interesting. Standing on tiptoe, Melissa reached up to the freshly shaven chin and planted a swift but teasing kiss on the astonished lips. 'It's such a heavenly morning, Gareth, don't you think?' she whispered, smiling at him with eyes that begged a warm invitation.

'What the...?' Gareth's voice trailed off as she turned quickly on her heel and darted along the narrow path that circumvented the garden and led to the kitchen door.

The last thing she wanted was to be confronted with Dian this morning. Hangovers were apt to recur given the right stimulation, but oh, how good she felt, playing Gareth at his own game. After last night she had no wish to be embroiled in their little forays, but the delicious surge of delight she had experienced just then was well worth the risk!

Reaching the safety of the kitchen and giving Susie her bowl of milk, Melissa reviewed the situation. Gareth would be hard put to it to explain the kiss ... and while he was under Dian's interrogation she would escape to the surgery.

Opening the kitchen door, Melissa froze where she stood. Guilt must have coloured her face, for the slender body clad in a beautiful kimono-style housecoat stiffened in front of her. 'Don't think you're going to get off so easily this time!' Dian hissed between beautifully glossed lips. 'You had everyone at the table yesterday to support you ... but you haven't now!'

'I don't know what you're talking about!'

Melissa jumped as icy shivers played along her spine, coal-dark eyes rooting her to the spot.

'You know exactly what I'm talking about – and I'm telling you – hands off! Gareth might like to give the impression that he's a free spirit, but he isn't. It might interest you to know that he proposed to me in Australia – and I turned him down. But when he left – and he left because he thought I wasn't interested in him – I realised I'd made a mistake.'

'Then perhaps you ought to be telling all this to Gareth,' Melissa responded, sticking out her small chin bravely.

'I have,' Dian said silkily. 'And we've decided to get married. Now do you understand?'

Melissa felt the blood drain from her face, experienced the awful turmoil of humiliation crimson her cheeks. All the time Gareth had led her on, all the time he had allowed her to think he really found her attractive … simply because he was on the rebound!

Knowing if she stayed any longer she would burst into tears, she fled from the kitchen, pushing past Dian, remembering with hindsight Dian's abrupt departure yesterday. It hadn't taken her long to get her own back!

Hurrying to the stairs, Melissa ran up the

three flights, her eyes blurring with tears she longed to shed in the privacy of her own room. But to her greater humiliation as she arrived on the top landing she ran directly into Gareth, changed now in his white coat for work. She tried to slip past him, but large, tanned hands reached out to grip her.

'Running into my arms again? Have you no pride?' he mocked cruelly. 'Now, shall we finish what you started in the garden a few minutes ago?'

Melissa shook him off, her grey eyes stinging with wetness. 'Leave me alone, Gareth! Once and for all, just leave me alone!'

Feeling her struggle in his arms, he muttered in sudden alarm, 'What on earth's the matter with you, girl. Stop and talk to me!'

'Nothing's the matter!' Melissa cried, telling herself she hated him. 'Please let me go, I have to get ready for work.'

'Forget work for a minute – what in heaven's name is going on with you? Yesterday evening you were all sweetness and light. This morning you bit my head off – then you kissed me. What the hell are you playing at, Melissa?'

She gasped, choking back her outrage. If only she could say she had heard them coming in … heard their laughter and excitement … heard them laughing behind her back at some silly joke at her expense!

And after Dian's revelation – what did he take her for? Was she wearing a placard saying 'Fool for hire!'?

Impetuously she retaliated, 'You might as well know, Gareth, I'm … I'm giving in my notice. I've thought about it – and I'm quite sure. So please don't try and change my mind … you won't have any difficulty in finding a replacement. Not with the incentives you'll provide.'

The spiteful sexual innuendo rang crisply on the quiet landing; even Melissa could not believe she had said it – but wasn't it true? Any prospective employee of the Tremaines would be treated to an enticing chunk of Gareth's undoubted charm, provided she had the right physical qualifications, and provided Dian wasn't within earshot of his nefarious flirtations.

Gareth's lips curled angrily, but his voice still held its steady resonance as he grated, 'It's a pity you couldn't have told me this before. Dad's just rung, and they're taking another couple of weeks in Scotland. I must say you've picked your time nicely!'

'I … I'm sorry about that,' Melissa croaked, 'but I think it's best for all concerned.'

'You do, do you? And would it be an inconvenience for you to explain your reasons? After all, I think it's only fair that you should provide at least one plausible excuse for running out on us just when we needed you the most.'

'That's not fair, Gareth! I've given your father every possible consideration – I'd never intentionally let him down!'

'But you'll let me down, is that it? Was I right in the first instance? It is money, isn't it?' he demanded. 'Tell me, just how much have you been offered to transfer your so-called loyalties? Or are you thinking of making that flight back with Peter when he goes?' His face contorted with suspicion. 'Ah, I can see I'm nearer to the truth there!'

They stared at one another, locked in mutual antipathy, Melissa mesmerised by the stubborn chin supporting the curl of lips hypocritically accusing her of double dealing! She had a mind to tell him exactly what she thought of his little games, his treacherous scheming! But something held her back ... possibly the insistent ringing of the phone in her room and the livid expression that was now flooding Gareth's once calm face.

'Well?' he muttered stonily, releasing her. 'Aren't you going to answer it ... or have you already quit?'

Melissa turned on her heel, shaking inside like a leaf. She walked into her bedroom, considering fleetingly the jug and hand basin again. Biting her bottom lip and refraining from the temptation, she picked up the small white receiver on the bedside table.

'Tremaine veterinary practice.'

The voice on the other end of the line left her in no doubt at all as to who it was. 'Mr Stopes,' she called with hostile intonation, covering the mouthpiece with her hand. 'He wants you. Do you want to take it here?'

'I wouldn't dare,' answered Gareth with a wry twist of the mouth. 'Switch it through to the office!'

Melissa watched the dark, forbidding figure vanish from sight and pressed the button to hold the call. Gareth had had the last word as usual, he'd even managed to throw in some pretty convincing accusations. Well, Dian and he were welcome to one another. They made a fine pair. On their wedding-day she might even send a telegram of good luck. For a couple so well matched in temperament would surely need it!

'What you're describing, Mr Stopes,' Gareth continued after a momentary lapse in concentration, 'is wet lamb hypothermia, and if he's only a few hours old you'll have to work quickly.' His face darkened as he watched Melissa walk across the room. 'I don't know how much it's going to cost. Do you want me to come out or not?'

Melissa couldn't even bring herself to feel annoyed at Mr Stopes's miserliness. Nothing seemed particularly important now. Perversely, her love had only crystallised for certain when she discovered it could not be returned. She blinked her eyes as she sat at the computer screen and tried to focus the details.

'Very well, I'll come ... but bring the lamb inside. No, the barn won't do ... the house, preferably. Thoroughly dry him. Have you an electric air heater? Good. Aim for a temperature of forty degrees Centigrade or a hundred degrees Fahrenheit.'

Gareth finally put down the phone, sighing. 'Stopes bought himself a couple of ewes. One of them's had a difficult parturition and the lamb's turning a nasty colour. The ewe, predictably, won't have anything to do with it.' He glanced at Melissa. 'I shall have to get over there ... hopefully I'll be back before surgery at ten-thirty. Walter's not coming in, is he?'

Melissa hardly allowed her eyes to leave the screen, not trusting herself to look into Gareth's face. Then, repenting because she knew he had the lamb's interest at heart and had relegated his own personal feelings of anger towards her, she answered, 'No, but I'll manage. I've got a number of another vet if an emergency crops up. What will you need? I'll pack the equipment for you while you have breakfast.'

Gareth stood still, his face showing the

same lines of tension which had so melted her yesterday, the lines she had longed to erase with her fingertips, and the memory of the ride in the Land Rover suddenly washed over her, making Dian's disclosure this morning seem heartbreakingly unbelievable.

'I'll need a couple of two hundred millilitre stomach tubes, an assortment of syringes and that spare heat lamp we keep for emergencies in the recovery-room,' Gareth went on. 'I'll probably have to give it an intravenous injection of glucose too.'

'How old is the lamb?' asked Melissa, making herself concentrate.

He shrugged, his eyes gentler now as he surveyed her. 'Newborn, Stopes thinks. But he's not very conversant with sheep, so he keeps telling me.'

Melissa got up from her seat and, forgetting the squall of temper which had boiled so recently inside her, said with lowered eyes, 'I'll see you have everything.'

There was a brief, dreadful silence, Gareth seemingly unwilling to leave the office.

'You'd better hurry,' she said dismissively, terrified he might try to persuade her to stay for his own convenience and even more terrified she might foolishly agree. But seconds later she heard his footsteps vanish down the hallway.

She sat numbly for a while, hardly able to

think. Then, realising she had work to do, she hurried to the dispensary and began to prepare the necessary equipment.

Ten minutes later she watched the Land Rover drive out of the car park. Feeling exhausted, she slumped into a chair. The morning had hardly begun, and already her whole life had changed ... irrevocably.

She was out of a job.

She had lost the opportunity of the vacancy in London by now. And she was suffering from the hangover again ... but this time she knew exactly what had caused it!

Gareth returned mid-morning to a busy surgery, and at lunchtime he asked Melissa to enter the details of the Stopes case as he read them out. 'The lamb was ten hours old at least...'

Melissa's slim fingers flew over the keyboard.

'Temperature, a degree Fahrenheit below normal, lamb starving, glucose injected into the abdominal cavity.' She looked up and saw his strained expression as he continued, 'Stomach tube feeding essential until ewe is prepared to feed.'

She completed the records, asking, 'Will Mr Stopes be able to cope with the feeding, do you think?'

Gareth gave her a heartwarming smile,

one which made her lose track of everything, including the file she had opened on her machine. 'I left him getting used to a sixty ml syringe. He's doing quite well, surprisingly. And while I was there I checked the mare and her foal. They're fine ... looking healthy. Stopes seems to be turning over a new leaf.'

Melissa gazed at the darkly lashed green eyes and felt her heart bounce crazily. Even Alfred Stopes and all his problems brought back a tingling memory...

'Hadn't you better switch that thing off?' Gareth suggested.

Melissa fumbled for the switch, feeling clumsy in his presence. She ached to lean on him ... he was so close, just a breath away. The solid warmth of his body was already reaching her chilled limbs, but with a tiny shudder she drew away, finally extinguishing the screen light.

'Melissa, you and I need to talk. We've got an hour or so...'

The phone rang insistently and with a muted curse Gareth strolled to pick it up. As she tidied her desk, Melissa listened to the sound of his voice, a voice which stirred such complicated and unknown feelings within her.

'Tomorrow ... that's not terribly convenient...'

She watched the firm mouth, the white

teeth grit themselves as he spoke, and felt her heart leap irrationally.

'I'll see what I can do, but I can't promise. I'll need an extra driver, and at the moment we're short-handed.'

Gareth replaced the receiver just as Peter entered the office, looking casually smart in light cords and a bright sunshine-coloured sweater. 'G'day!'

Gareth nodded his good morning, obviously restrained. Peter glanced furtively at Melissa, raising his blond eyebrows. 'I wondered if you fancied a sandwich at the local, Melissa... Gareth, can you get away too?'

Gareth's eyes made her shiver with their cold brilliance as he dismissed Peter's offer. 'No, thanks. I've a bit to catch up on here. Don't let that stop you, though, Melissa,' he said bitingly.

Melissa chewed on her bottom lip as she instinctively opened her mouth to refuse Peter. But why should she? What reason was there to hang around the surgery? If she did, Gareth would only try to make her change her mind for purely selfish reasons. And if Dian was to arrive, all hell would probably be let loose. This seemed the perfect excuse to avoid either unpleasant alternative.

'I'd like that, Peter,' she smiled. 'Can you give me five minutes and I'll be with you?'

As she left the room she was suddenly aware of Gareth's obvious animosity. His wide mouth seemed to be twitching, and there was an arrogant, belligerent stance about him that made the hairs on the back of her neck prickle.

She was glad she was going out with Peter. At least there was someone in the house who seemed to have retained their sanity.

But Melissa was to realise just how wrong she was when, as she sat in the Queen's Head with Peter, he suddenly covered her hand with his own and asked her to fly back to Australia with him.

CHAPTER TEN

'But we hardly know each other, Peter!'

'I know enough to ask you to consider my offer ... very seriously,' said Peter, taking the small fingers between his large hands and looking earnestly at her.

The Queen's Head buzzed with lunchtime activity. Melissa's head buzzed with something quite different – shock, she supposed, at Peter's stunning suggestion.

'Don't you think we'd make a good team? I've watched you carefully this last week, Melissa. You're efficient, thorough, versatile ... and unattached. Surely you'd like to travel, wouldn't you, see new places, meet people? I could guarantee you a wonderful new experience...'

'In exchange for what?' Melissa looked doubtfully at the blond, blue-eyed Australian sitting beside her trying so hard to persuade her to make a radical change in her life.

'No strings, I promise. There's plenty of scope for women with drive and enthusiasm in Australia, especially in my line of business. You can handle the technology, you're fantastic with people. What prospects does this job offer you? Come on, be honest with me!'

Precisely none at this moment, Melissa thought, avoiding Peter's gaze. In fact, she was virtually jobless, and as far as her commitments at home went, Gramps seemed to be taking on a whole new lease of life with Eileen Purdy. Wasn't this as good a time as any to make changes in her life?

She turned her grey eyes on the expectant blue ones gazing at her. 'I'm a veterinary nurse, Peter. There's something about this job ... working with animals, I suppose, that makes any other kind of work seem unfulfilling; it's hard to put it into words really. Your offer is marvellously attractive...'

Peter shrugged his wide shoulders. 'Can you expect me to believe our four-legged friends mean that much to you?' And before Melissa could stop him, he leant towards her and kissed her, whispering, 'Does this help to convince you? I really do think we could make a go of things together.'

Melissa jumped as she sampled an unexpected warmth and a tenderness, even a little flutter, at the urgency of his lips. But as he drew away, she could only see one face before her. Green eyes reproving her, dark hair swathed back to lie on a strong neck, the haunting image of an Englishman she couldn't forget no matter how much she tried, making her soul seem empty at the other man's touch.

Finding it hard to answer him without hurting his feelings, she explained, 'That's precisely it, Peter. I like you a lot, and it would be unfair of me to let you think it was anything more.'

'If it's love you're talking about,' Peter said flatly, 'isn't that a rather old-fashioned concept in this day and age?'

Melissa sighed, knowing what he said might possibly be true – for some people! 'This sounds silly, I know, Peter, but I always promised myself I'd wait for the right person to come along. Perhaps I'll go on waiting until I'm a dithering old spinster, but I believe in love, you see. Stupid, I know, but I don't think I could make a commitment unless I was absolutely sure.'

'Then don't,' Peter said quickly. 'Don't make any promises. I'm not asking for more than you can give.'

She shook her head, stunned. 'I'm flattered ... even a little tempted, but–'

'Don't decide now,' he told her. 'I'm driving Dian up to London on Saturday, she's got an assignment arranged at the weekend for a magazine. Thursday I'm flying home. I want you on the plane with me.'

He kissed her again in the car.

She seemed hardly to have any choice as he brought her to him like a tiny doll, forcing the breath out of her body. The kiss was more like an act of aggression, the strong hands rounded her shoulders, ruckling the thin material of her dress and sliding down to the full, round curve of her breast.

'Peter ... Peter,' she begged, 'don't!'

He broke regretfully away. 'I'm ... sorry, Melissa. God, you had a strange effect on me then. I didn't know what I was doing!'

Melissa smiled, embarrassed, straightening herself out and brushing down her uniform.

'I suppose I'd better get you back, hadn't I?' he said regretfully, and as he plunged the BMW into first gear Melissa found her fingers trembling as she locked in her safety-belt.

Confronting Gareth when she returned felt more like confronting an irate father waiting on the doorstep. She blushed heavily as Peter gave her a friendly cuddle goodbye and left her to walk in.

'Thanks for being so prompt,' growled Gareth as she walked into his treatment-room, obviously having watched the little scene from his window. 'I don't need to ask if you had a good time!'

Melissa smoothed back her hair, feeling ridiculously guilty. 'I don't think that's any of your business.'

'It is when you're late and I have to open up myself.'

'Five minutes late.' Melissa glanced hastily at her watch. 'I'd hardly call it worth noticing.'

'You apparently don't notice very much at all lately,' Gareth returned sharply, handing her some equipment for sterilising, 'that isn't concerned with him.'

'What exactly do you mean?'

'He's been mooning around the house all week – and don't say you haven't encouraged him!'

Melissa's grey eyes flickered challengingly. 'And what if I have? Is it anything to do with you, Gareth?'

'So you admit it's true?' he demanded.

'Peter deserves all the attention he gets,' she answered quietly. 'He's always friendly and charming and polite.'

'Are you in love with him?'

Melissa almost dropped the forceps. She turned to stare at Gareth, who had walked towards her, his brows knitted in a deep pleat across his forehead.

'What did you say?' she gasped in astonishment.

He stared at her. 'I asked you if you were in love with him.'

'Why … why should I discuss my feelings for Peter? It's no concern of yours!'

'As it happens, it is,' Gareth answered her roughly, his closeness making her tremble. 'Answer me, are you in love with him?'

Melissa stared into the slanted eyes piercing her with such ferocity. 'Peter's just asked me…' She gulped, knowing with a dreadful certainty that in spite of her anger, Gareth's proximity was causing an embarrassing arousal of her body under the thin material of her dress. 'To … go to Australia with him.'

'And like a fool you accepted!'

He gave her no time to defend herself, for suddenly he had hold of her arms, causing the forceps to clatter noisily to the floor. 'So I was right all along…'

'No, you weren't!' Melissa cried out, unsure in her mind whether she was trying to save her integrity or the fickle body which was yielding under Gareth's powerful grip, knowing this was more than just a simple stir of sexual attraction.

She could have struggled but she didn't. A breathtaking tremor of excitement began in her solar plexus and travelled like a snake around her spine as Gareth's body pressed into hers.

'You've no right to question me like this,' she bleated lamely, trying to avert her gaze from the darkly handsome face.

He forced her attention back to him by shaking her, his lips curling angrily. 'Now listen to me! Peter isn't thinking straight … and you shouldn't lead him on! You're playing with fire, and I don't have to remind you again that you may very well get burned!'

'L-let go of me!' stammered Melissa, her heart jerking. 'How dare you?'

'I dare because I don't want to see you make a fool of yourself, even though you seem hell-bent on doing so. I didn't want to have to make this common knowledge because it's nobody's business but theirs … however, you might as well know, Peter brought Dian to England because he couldn't bear to let her out of his sight.'

'Peter's just a caring brother–'

'Not in the way you think.' Gareth's hold tightened, sending all her sensations into a frenzy.

'How can you say such a thing?' she gasped.

'Easily.' The resentment in the greeny eyes smouldered dangerously. 'He's her step-brother, not related by blood. His mother married her father when Peter and Dian were in their teens. The problem was that Peter doted on her from the very beginning … and Dian has always made the most of it. She makes the most of every man in her life … she never wastes them.'

A searing pain assailed Melissa just beneath her ribs. Gareth was talking like a rejected lover!

'Dian would never let him go, my darling little innocent; you're no match for her. Even if she didn't want him, she'd never let you have him.'

'And you expect me to believe such a … a ridiculous story?' she demanded.

'Believe what you like! I'm just warning you … you've got him fancying you like hell now. Dian thinks she stands to lose out, and you're proving a big threat to her. Do you think you could handle being Dian Taylor's sister-in-law?'

Melissa shrank at the very thought. She hadn't even considered it!

Gareth's darkening features loomed above her fair head as he brought her to him again.

'Just how far have things gone between you two?' he asked abruptly, squeezing her arms, his high cheekbones hollowing as he looked down at her.

Melissa could only stare blindly at him, her eyes growing wide as saucers. How could he think she would give herself to someone she'd only just met?

'You don't know me very well,' she whispered angrily, breathlessly protesting, her hands now against the swell of his firm chest, the wiry hairs matting the dark skin just discernible under her fingertips. Her whole body shuddered.

'I seem to remember saying something similar to you once,' said Gareth, his voice softer now, yet the urgency of the body under her touch shocked her with such force that she could hardly believe what was happening.

There was nothing slow or tentative about his kiss this time. It powered the sensations of need and of unbearable desire throughout her whole body, turning her limbs to water and her lips to fire. Dimly she realised that his hands were roving her body, forcing her hipbones into his own powerful physique so that she gasped and almost choked at the physical arousal they shared between them.

She arched into him, powerless to deny herself the pleasure. His kisses rained across her neck and down into the small hollow between her breasts where somehow her uniform seemed to have come unbuttoned. She realised with shock that she was beginning to know more about herself in this moment than in the whole of her lifetime as

218

her body ignited with a new and unquenchable flame.

'Gareth…' she whispered, hardly knowing what she was saying, feeling the touch of his hands travel her skull, pulling her mass of blonde hair back firmly, passionately, until, holding her steady and with fire on his lips, he kissed her again.

'My God, my darling,' he breathed, a scalding body pressing against her, 'what are you doing to me?'

'People … in Reception…' she began, her words dying under the fusion of their lips as his tongue teased her with the memory of that very first kiss in the garden. Her fingers and toes tingled with small electric shocks as she reached out in an agony of delight. His arms tightened again, refusing to let her go – refusing her breath even to turn her head upwards. Opening her lips, she hardly had strength to fight against the bruising enquiry of his mouth.

She loved him. Sweet heaven, she loved him, fool that she was!

He lit her with a fire that both consumed her and rebirthed her. A shudder of need convulsed her again and, all equilibrium lost, they fell heavily against the wall, Gareth's strong arms cushioning the hardness beneath her back. In the oblivion of what was happening, Melissa found her own fingers travelling the sensual hardness of his straight hips underneath the white jacket running down to the athletic thighs that pressed into her.

Amazed at herself, she removed her fingers, but some form of magnetism drew them back to pull his shirt teasingly from the leather belt.

Suddenly the sight of tanned, bare midriff, coils of hair spreading darkly upwards, made her gasp. Looking up, she met deep pools of ocean green drowning her with their enticement as he cupped her tiny waist, drawing her to him, allowing her the pleasure of his full enjoyment in her.

'You see exactly what you've done?' Spreading his arms and legs, he pinioned her against the wall, making her gasp for air. 'Now what are you going to do about the situation?' he asked her, his lips turning up in wry amusement.

Easing herself up on tiptoe, her breasts moulding themselves into his chest and capturing the drift of his aftershave as she turned her head upwards involuntarily to be kissed, she shuddered in delight as he sank down on her.

Neither of them registered the turning of the door-handle. Neither of them saw the tall, dark young woman walk into the room, her eyes fixing them with steel arrows.

'So this is what goes on in a veterinary's treatment-room! I always wondered,' scoffed

Dian, her voice startlingly crisp.

Gareth swivelled, his large body obscuring Melissa for one brief second. 'Dian, don't you believe in knocking first?' he grated, tucking in the dishevelled shirt.

Melissa blinked, realising for the first time in moments what had been happening to her. Caught on a wave of emotion, she had lost her senses! What had possessed her? With a waiting-room full of patients, tempting fate had certainly been the last thing on her mind.

Rearranging the small flap of her unbuttoned top, she tried to avoid Dian's thunderous glance.

'Just what's your little game?' Dian asked in acid-sweet tones, walking very slowly towards them.

Melissa stiffened her spine. 'Not a lot different from yours, I should imagine,' she defended hastily. 'At least from what I've heard!'

Dian's face creased cruelly, her black hair and red lips reminding Melissa of the Wicked Witch of the North come to claim her rightful prize.

'Ah, I see!' Dian muttered under her breath. 'Peter's been telling tales out of school, has he? I wondered as much when I came back from shopping today. But I thought you two were too occupied in slobbering over one another outside that little

221

pub in Dorlington to notice me – and I was right. That clinch in the car ... you little English rose creatures certainly don't mind being deflowered when the occasion calls for it!'

Melissa gasped, her breath catching as she looked at Gareth. Suddenly his whole demeanour changed. His lips were white and thin and his green eyes surveyed Dian with the coldness of ice, though he said nothing.

Dian had aimed her poisoned dart and it had hit perfectly home. For a moment the three of them stood locked in silence, Dian's lips quivering with the need to seal Melissa's immediate fate with more treachery.

'I think you'd better see to your clients, don't you?' muttered Gareth with an offhand shrug. 'And Dian, you'll have to run along and amuse yourself elsewhere for a while.'

'I want to talk to you, Gareth,' Dian told him, unwilling to be moved. 'I'm leaving for London with Peter the day after tomorrow and I want to settle a few dates with you. Important dates.'

Melissa's heart froze as Dian looked triumphantly at her. 'I don't think we need bother Melissa for anything further,' Dian purred sweetly, opening the door.

With her cheeks burning and humiliation gnawing at her bones, Melissa fled the room.

Walter Forbes, exhausted from his shopping trip with his wife, poked his head round the office door. 'Thought I'd catch you before you closed. Gareth phoned earlier and left a message that he wants me in a bit sharpish tomorrow. Do you know anything about it, Melissa?'

Melissa looked up from her work at the desk, work which had been blurring before her eyes for the past hour. The afternoon had been a disaster, with animals rampant in the waiting-room, a lost hamster chased and regained with difficulty and Gareth refusing to meet her glance as she helped him with their patients.

Now it was almost six, and before she closed the door for the evening she was trying to decipher some of Gareth's notes for computing. No doubt his mind had been too concerned with Dian's fixing of wedding bells to bother to write legibly!

'He's going off to collect his new vehicle, I understand,' Walter told her, coming in and lighting his pipe.

'Is he?' Then Melissa suddenly remembered the phone call and Gareth explaining that he was short-handed. 'I'm afraid I don't know the exact details. Shall I call Gareth for you? He's in with his last client.'

'No, not to worry. Just tell him I'll be here at eight-thirty, will you?'

Melissa nodded. 'A second vehicle …

goodness! I didn't know Gordon had even considered one.'

'He hasn't,' Walter advised her, perching on the edge of her desk and blowing a fog across the room. 'It's going to be a surprise. That old boneshaker of his needs a complete overhaul.'

Melissa looked blankly at him. 'A surprise?' she echoed.

Walter nodded, winking. 'Organised by Gareth. He's got big plans for this practice, you know. Got to give the boy credit. Thought he'd start off by getting decent transport for his father.'

Melissa blinked, unable for the moment to comprehend what she was being told. Gareth was as poor as a church mouse as far as she knew. How could he afford a new vehicle?

As though reading her mind, Walter added, 'Not one to boast, is our Gareth. Made considerable investments in Aussie, made good … just like he said he was going to. When he found out that his father was having a hard time of it, he came home. More or less saved Gordon from bankruptcy.'

'I … I had no idea, Walter… I always thought Gordon and Rose were solvent!' gasped Melissa.

'They were … until the remodernisation took every penny they had. Technology costs a small fortune these days. Blasted bank called in their loan before Gordon had a chance to get his bearings.'

Suddenly everything fell into place in Melissa's mind. The wonderful plans Gordon had had to extend which had been put on hold, the new operating theatre and computers, their laboratory... She had thought it mere running out of steam due to Gordon's age, but it had been pressure of financial worries! What a fool she was not to realise! She was so preoccupied with her own problems, keeping her grandfather and herself under one roof, that she hadn't dreamt Gordon and Rose were in dire straits.

'Look,' Walter said worriedly, viewing her surprise, 'I'm a bit of an old blabbermouth. I'd appreciate if it you didn't mention that I'd told you all this, Melissa. It's a question of pride, you see, with Gordon and Rose. Especially at their ages ... having to have their son come home and bail them out.'

Melissa nodded slowly. 'I wouldn't dream of saying a word, Walter. But I'm glad you mentioned it. Sometimes one gets too bogged down with one's own troubles to notice others'.'

Walter shifted creakily from the desk. 'You're a good lass, Melissa. Like a daughter to the Tremaines. Don't suppose they wanted to worry you, not with your grandfather ... how is the old rascal, by the way?'

'Fine, thanks.' Melissa smiled gratefully at him, mentally kicking herself for being so blind. Money had been Gareth's reason for returning to England, but to give it, not to take it!

After Walter had gone, she locked the door and slipped along to Gareth's treatment-room, her heart thudding crazily. How wrong she had been about him ... and it mattered dreadfully. She would confess her suspicions, try to put right the bad feeling between them...

She opened his door.

An empty room met her eyes.

She crossed the floor and peeped between the blinds. In the shadowy sunlight evening, Beetle romped on the lawn with Susie. Dian and Gareth stood beneath the trees, her beautiful face upturned towards him. Delicately he stroked her cheek.

Melissa watched, too shocked by her own sense of utter disappointment to move.

Finally she walked from the room. What a fool she had been! What a stupid, idiotic, childish fool!

Melissa woke at seven. She felt an instant dread, the gnawing at the base of her stomach that shouted, 'Fool, fool!'

She swung her slim legs from the bed and eased on her robe. Going to the window, she looked down to see Gareth attending to the Land Rover. With his dark head bent over the engine he was too engrossed to notice her. She savoured every movement, watching the long, powerful back move gracefully, like an animal over its prey. She shuddered, remembering his kisses yesterday, the hands attempting to catch hold of her, the supple body against her own.

She tore herself away from the window. Dian would soon be climbing into the Land Rover beside him. Gareth wouldn't risk leaving Dian alone now. He would take her with him to collect the new vehicle, serving the dual purpose of collection and keeping his fiancée out of harm's way.

What a depressing day it was going to be! She hoped Peter would make himself scarce ... she just couldn't face him today of all days. Though perhaps Australia wasn't such a bad idea now...

'Morning, Melissa!' Mrs Carter met her in the kitchen just as she was coming in the door. 'Beautiful day ... going to be a fine one.'

Melissa smiled. Fine for some people, but not for her.

'Gareth's trying to breathe new life into that noisy old crate,' Mrs Carter told her, taking off her coat and rolling up her sleeves. 'A long journey, too. Don't fancy it at all, I don't! Still, it'll make a welcome change seeing Grace today. We'll be able to have a nice chinwag about old times, she being Mrs T's best friend.'

'Grace?' asked Melissa abstractedly, pouring muesli into her bowl.

'Grace Forbes, Walter's wife – you know.'

'Why would Grace be coming over?' asked Melissa, prodding her breakfast without enthusiasm.

Mrs Carter turned around, adjusting her pinafore, her small eyes screwing up. 'What's the matter with you lately, my girl? Honestly, the household's gone mad since the Tremaines have been away! Walter won't be able to manage on his own now, will he?'

'But I'm here,' Melissa murmured, confounded.

'News to me!' Mrs Carter turned a sharp knife to a potato. 'You're off with His Nibs!'

Melissa's spoon stopped its stirring. Her grey eyes travelled up the ramrod back of Mrs Carter to the grey bun. 'I'm not going with Gareth … am I?' she queried.

Mrs Carter smiled to herself, though the young woman at the table could not see her amusement. She merely said, 'You'd better go and see for yourself, hadn't you?'

'Glastonbury!' gasped Melissa. 'But that's miles away!'

Gareth shrugged. 'Does it make any difference? Or did you want to hang around for your … friend? If so, you're going to have a long wait. He left at six sharp this morning.'

Melissa watched his nimble fingers doing

something with little bits under the engine. 'He wasn't going until tomorrow,' she argued perversely.

Gareth straightened his spine, wiping oily fingers on a cloth. 'Well, he's gone today! Have you any objections?'

His tone made her bristle. 'It's not up to me to have any objections. Peter can do as he likes!'

'Very generous of you!'

'There's no need to be facetious, Gareth. I was just surprised. I thought you'd be taking Dian.'

A wry smile edged Gareth's lips as he bent over the engine again. 'You thought wrong again. Dian isn't available. She went with Peter. It's Hobson's choice, I'm afraid. Either you come with me or we don't take possession of the vehicle, which will be ... damn it ... most inconvenient!' He cursed as his hand slipped, and looked up angrily. 'Well? If you're coming, you'd better wear something presentable, a dress or something ... we're going to a main dealer. I don't want them to think we're out of the Dark Ages!'

Dark Ages my foot! thought Melissa, her relief suddenly turning to fury. Hobson's choice, was she? She clenched her small fists and counted to ten. Something presentable, he wanted, did he? Well, she had exactly the right outfit to suit her mood and his!

Furiously she turned away, striding

towards the house with her freckles glowing luminously.

'And you've got exactly thirty minutes until Walter and Grace arrive. So don't fiddle around unnecessarily – be on time!' came the fierce instruction behind her.

Teeth clenched, fists in a ball, Melissa stormed into the house. Who in heaven's name did he think he was, to speak to her in such a way? She hated him. She really hated him! He would never have dared to treat Dian like that – considering the time it took to paint a mural on her face each morning!

Fifteen minutes later exactly, Melissa scrutinised herself in the mirror.

Perfect! Placing tiny glittering stars in her ears and a simple gold chain around her neck, combined with heels which gave her an added inch, she stood, her temper cooling.

Black was rather a shock to the system.

Her funeral suit, as she named it, might be designer-made, but together with her hair coiled up into a svelte chignon, did she emulate Dian rather too closely for comfort?

She had intended to make Gareth eat his words ... 'a dress or something'. Did he think she lived in a green nurse's uniform? Did he think she couldn't be sophisticated if she wanted?

Trembling at her own unfamiliar reflection, she tried a smile. It came out lopsided. She tried again, practising her demure appearance. Giving up all hope after her third effort, she collected her bag and nervously began the trip downstairs.

Having made the journey unnoticed to the front door, opening it quietly, she came face to face with four very surprised people.

Only one of them made a remark.

Mrs Carter, folding her chubby arms across her breast and using her most unsuitable mixed metaphors, sniffed, 'My goodness me! Stone the crows if we don't have a dose of the cat's whiskers today!'

CHAPTER ELEVEN

Rumbling along in the Land Rover, Melissa gritted her teeth, feeling ridiculously over-dressed. The feeling grew as the bumpy ride sprang a couple of grips from her chignon, one curly lock of hair bouncing down on to her nose.

It was all Gareth's fault!

At least Grace and Walter had had the decency not to laugh as Gareth, with that infuriatingly smug smile of his, had hoisted her in, the question of her climbing up herself decided by the pencil-slim skirt and its restrictive width.

For the first time since they began the

journey Melissa removed her seething glance from the road and looked down at her watch. An hour gone. And not a word spoken!

That suited her fine. She didn't want to speak to him … she hated him. He probably hadn't dared to ask Dian to go with him today … would she sit on a hard seat for hours on end, clinging on for dear life every time they rounded a corner?

When the vehicle swerved viciously and Melissa slid helplessly across to find herself clinging on to Gareth, she was no less surprised by his growled 'Hell's bells!' than the fact that they were facing the oncoming traffic – in the middle of the road!

'A flat!' Gareth exclaimed, fighting with the steering-wheel.

Melissa registered briefly the strong male arm which had automatically flung itself across her at the impact of the crunching halt, and a shiver tingled the nape of her neck, making the fine hairs stand on end as she felt his touch.

Gareth glanced in his driving mirror. 'Lucky our speed was down or we'd have been in trouble. Are you all right?'

She nodded, feeling a further collapse of the superstructure of her hair already beginning to tumble about her face.

'I'll pull in over there,' he told her as he wrenched the steering-wheel round and jerkingly they wobbled their way on to the safety of the grass verge. 'Soon have her back on the road.'

Melissa doubted the word 'soon'. As far as she knew, tyre changing wasn't always a straightforward process – nothing to do with cars ever was! It involved a lot of grease and oil and huffing and puffing, and men always seemed to end up throwing things about before actually remedying the problem.

'I've full confidence in you,' she said drily, sitting back to relax and crossing her long legs for the first time, since for the last sixty minutes she had had to have both feet safely planted on the floor to steady herself. At least now she could attend to the more important business of rearranging her disorderly locks. She opened her bag and drew out a hand mirror.

'You won't need that,' Gareth told her abruptly as he got out of the driver's side. 'Not where you're going! We've work to do.'

Shock and disbelief shadowed Melissa's face as he strode round to her door and propelled her on to the grass verge.

He guided her to the back of the Land Rover, pulled a dirty spray can from a wooden box and stuck it in her hand. 'This is a cleaner, a very effective one. When I give you some small round objects called nuts, I want you to spray them. Here's a cloth – make sure they aren't encrusted with farmyard muck first.'

Melissa glared at the pitiful rag and the grease-covered spray soiling her hands. 'You've got to be joking!' she gasped in horror. 'I can't do that ... I'm not dressed for it!'

'I didn't ask you to wear something out of *Vogue*,' Gareth muttered, and was gone, assembling tools beside the flat tyre.

She hurried after him, her slim heels digging into the soft earth. 'Of all the cheek! You specifically asked me to wear–'

'Watch out, you're in the way of the jacking point.' Gareth waved a spanner at her and she jumped back, pivoting on a heel.

The crack mingled with the jacking noise and Gareth's deep sigh of impatience. 'Now what are you doing?' he shouted over his shoulder as she toppled to one side.

'My heel's snapped!' Melissa almost choked at the sight of her heel sticking up from the ground like a headless mushroom. 'My best shoes!'

Gareth made some unintelligible noise and peered under the vehicle, the familiar posterior, the one she had discovered protruding from her Mini two weeks ago, raised temptingly towards her.

'Did you hear me, Gareth?' she cried in exasperation, instructing herself to put all thoughts out of her head that even verged on physical appreciation of the male form – especially this male form. 'I should never have agreed to come… I must have been out of my mind!'

A large wet globule landed on her nose as Gareth appeared from the underside. More blobs followed as, completely ignoring her, he began furiously winding the nuts from the jacked wheel.

'It's raining!' Melissa burst out.

'You don't say.' Gareth threw her a small oil-crusted object. 'That's the first nut. They're coming off easily enough, a little rusty – but if you look in my toolbox you'll find some sandpaper. Just give them a dust over.'

Melissa stared in disbelief as the hard metal object landed on her sleeve and bounced from her hip to her hem, blazing a slimy trail behind it. As it fell into the grass at her feet, she stared open-mouthed as Gareth muttered, 'Butterfingers!'

'My new suit…!' Her voice trailed off disbelievingly.

'There's some grease remover in the back … look sharp, here's two more nuts.'

'If you think I'm going anywhere near that filthy box–' Melissa defiantly folded her slim arms across her chest, until a fresh downpour of rain completely soaked her.

Miserably picking up the motley assortment, she trudged to the back of the Land Rover and climbed aboard to attack the toolbox.

An hour later, installed in the front seat again, she could hardly believe she had actually done what Gareth had told her to … cleaned, sandpapered, and broken a nail into the bargain … and drowned in the rain!

When Gareth appeared beside her, his dark hair curling at the ears and rain dripping from his nose, he shook himself like a dog emerging from the sea, beaming her a smile.

'Great job!' came the sigh of satisfaction.

Melissa was too furious to reply. Couldn't he see the state she was in?

'Just a minute!' He reached into the back seat. 'I've got a towel at the back here.'

She stared at her black hands lying in her oil-stained lap. A towel wasn't going to help! Swirls of navy oil interlaced with dark brown mud streaked the front of her skirt. Her knees were filthy. Her one good shoe graced a grimy ankle and a soaked calf. She dared not think about her hair … the fact that it was hanging in ringlets around her ears as it always did when it got wet reminded her of the fact that she had worn mascara to complement her hair-style. Peering into her hand mirror, she saw one black eye and uttered a shriek.

'Don't panic,' came the calm instruction beside her, 'I've got a blanket here.'

Melissa began her count to ten, shivering

236

with such ferocity that she stopped at five, her lips quivering with anger as well as cold.

'Take those wet things off,' Gareth told her calmly, 'and put this around you.'

Melissa heard her own strangled voice as though it was coming from another world. 'Just … just look at me … look what you've done! I don't want your stupid blanket! I … I want to go home! Now!'

For the first time since climbing into the Land Rover Gareth seemed to appreciate the devastation in the form of a drowned, dirty female sitting beside him. His eyes, at first seriously appraising her, slowly widened and to her unutterable humiliation his mouth turned up at the corners and despite his obvious effort to control himself he began laughing, his whole face creasing up as the sound of his laughter echoed in Melissa's wet ears.

Her fury broke with half-muted sobs. 'I hate you, Gareth Tremaine! I hate you and despise you – and I never want to see you again – ever!'

She swung open her door, not having an earthly what she was going to do. Some sort of idiotic idea was forming in the back of her mind. She would wave down a car … hitch a lift … walk to the nearest town if she had to!

Enough was enough.

She was mad to think she could have ever

been in love with him! He had somehow had a strange power over her emotions, but today the spell was broken. Whatever it was she felt for him did not add up to love … or even like!

'Don't touch me!' she yelled as a hand caught the elbow of her soggy sleeve and she wrenched it away fiercely. Slamming the door behind her, she pulled herself up to her full five feet six … it would have been vastly more impressive if she'd had two decent heels to stand on and hair which hadn't taken on the shape of a well used mop, but nevertheless, narrowing her eyes, she glared proudly through the misted window.

'Go back and ask your precious friend from Australia to help you out… I'm sure she won't mind acting as stand-in mechanic for you!' she snapped.

She stalked off, lopsidedly. She threw back her wet shoulders, ignoring the fresh surge of rain, and headed … she didn't know where, but as far away as possible from the man who was still laughing at her even now.

The image of the sparkling green eyes caused her to quicken her step – misguidedly. In doing so she tripped on the good heel, sinking deeply into the rain-soaked mud. Wrenching off both shoes, she threw them into the ditch.

The rain thundered down, but she told herself not to look back – she didn't care, all she had in her heart was hate at this particular moment for a man who had the sensitivity of a bulldozer!

At least his plans to collect his precious vehicle were thwarted. What was he going to do? Go back and collect Dian? Hardly. Models modelled on yachts and expensive motor cars and tropical islands; they didn't spend hours driving tanks! If Gareth imagined Dian was going to soil one little finger in the course of helping him, he had rather a nasty shock coming to him!

A lorry loomed in the distance and Melissa bravely stuck out her thumb. The last time she had hitch-hiked was in her teens on the Continent, and if she remembered rightly lorry drivers were always accommodating ... though naturally enough there were always stories about women disappearing...

Melissa's hand wavered in mid-air.

The lorry grumbled to a halt, its driver leaning across and poking his unshaven face through the window. 'Where you heading, darlin'?' The door flew open and a giant of a man gazed down on her.

Melissa gulped. 'I ... I...'

'She's heading right back where she belongs ... with me!' Gareth swung her towards him, his face rain-soaked and angry. 'You little fool! What the hell do you think you're doing?'

'Let me go!' shouted Melissa, struggling.

The burly lorry driver leaned out of his cab. 'You all right, love? He bothering you?'

Gareth grasped her tightly around the waist, cupping her chin in his wet hand and kissing her roughly. 'Just a small difference of opinion – isn't that right, darling?'

Melissa opened her mouth to disagree, and Gareth kissed her again. His slow sensuous touch over her wet body caused minute shocks to travel her skin. Goosebumps and summer rain mixed together, streaking down their faces and into the heat of the kiss.

Neither of them heard the lorry driver's curse, nor the rumble of the huge tyres as he trundled off. Melissa was only aware that Gareth's lips were causing her state of helpless confusion to turn into a most desperate need, a euphoria which transcended the wet and the dirt and the soggy ground on which she was standing barefoot. His fingers slid down her cheeks, flickered across her throat, entangled themselves with her drenched hair.

'You silly, silly girl!' she heard as his arms enfolded her closer. Bewildered, she watched the hard symmetry of his face change as he gazed at her. His cheek came down softly on hers as they stood in the rain, Melissa's heart racing until she felt it would burst. With joy, with happiness, with sadness, with disappointment – she had no idea. Perhaps it was all these things at once, in the arms of the man she could not stop loving; no matter what she told herself, no matter how much he taunted her, she was crazy enough to be clinging to him now, knowing she hadn't an ounce of will-power left to fight him.

'Now be quiet,' he told her, laying a wet finger across her lips. 'Don't argue, don't complain – you may blow your nose if you like, but that's all, do you understand?'

Melissa nodded meekly as without a word more he swept her up into his arms, carrying her like a child through the torrent of rain, her arms about his neck, the whispers of his dark hair dripping on to her slim wrists.

Reaching the Land Rover, he kissed her again, a long slow kiss unaided by the expertise of his hands which still supported her small weight. Her lips felt extraordinarily sensitive as she peeped to watch the thick lashes quiver in response to her slightly parted mouth.

Slowly he set her down, opened the door and lifted her in – back from the place from which she had fled in anger. Back ten times as wet and filthy. But back beside him and unable to do anything about it because of her weak, vulnerable self!

Gareth climbed in beside her. He was

soaking wet too, his thin sweater clinging to the firm, muscular smoothness of his body and making her catch her breath in surprise. How was it that every time she looked at him she found something new, something wonderful about him to tease her emotions?

'Take off your clothes,' he commanded, suddenly jolting her out of her daydreaming. 'And I'm not going to seduce you here on the roadside, so don't look at me like that. Strip off, and wrap this round you.'

Melissa stared for a second, considering the alternatives. There were none. He was being sensible – which was more than she had been! The blanket looked warm and cosy and she was shivering from head to toe. Slowly she began to peel off her jacket. Two large hands came to her rescue as the drenched fabric stuck to her skin.

'Now the dress,' Gareth told her firmly. 'Turn round and I'll unzip you.'

Melissa's grey eyes nearly popped out of her head. 'I … I can manage…'

'No, you can't – and stop dithering!'

He spun her round in her seat and wriggled the zip to the base of her spine.

Melissa gasped at the sensation it drove through her body, his fingers fleetingly touching her skin. As she slipped the dress over her shoulders and manoeuvred it shyly down her body, her cheeks flared at the way he was looking at her. Her silky bra and panties were soaked, her bare brown legs shiny, but surely he didn't intend her to remove her undies too?

Gareth raised a dark eyebrow, his handsome face regarding her with obvious admiration. For fleeting seconds Melissa hadn't a clue what she should do with her hands, her high, well rounded breasts heaving helplessly under the raging male scrutiny, covered only by the scanty bra.

The moment was filled with indecision.

She knew that if he touched her she would be powerless to refuse him, such were her feelings at this very moment. The man she distrusted, the man who had humiliated her, was stirring in her body such treacherous desire that she felt breathless and heady. Hurriedly she glanced away, reaching out for the blanket which he held in his hands.

'Afraid, Melissa?' he asked her huskily as she tried to wrap herself, her nakedness becoming painfully obvious. 'Afraid to admit to your real feelings for once?'

'No!' she blurted, feeling as though he could look right through her mind. 'Just frozen!'

Leaning towards her, he draped the blanket round her shoulders. 'Please take me home,' she implored, tears beginning to blur her eyes, the thought of his close proximity and her absurd fantasies cruelly tugging at her heart.

'That's the last place I'm going to take you,' he answered severely. 'Whether you like it or not, you're going to listen to a few home truths ... clothes or no clothes!'

'Wait here – and don't move!' Gareth warned her as he jumped out of the Land Rover to disappear into the courtyard entrance of an old hotel. Melissa peered upwards to a sign hanging from a beam which read 'The Balmoral'.

She huddled into the blanket, steaming. If she hadn't been so miserable, so tired and so hungry, she would have appreciated the quaint little Glastonbury streets through which they had just passed, freshly washed with rain. But when you were sickening for pneumonia and hadn't had a morsel in your stomach all day, and when your body longed only to soak in a sizzlingly hot bath, admiring the scenery was a long way down the list of priorities!

What Gareth was doing now she had no idea – perhaps he was phoning the distributors to explain why they were late. But if he imagined she was going to drive all the way back to Dorlington in a blanket...!

'With compliments from the management.' Gareth opened her door and handed her a towelling robe. 'Change into it here and I'll smuggle you upstairs in the service lift.'

Melissa looked blankly at the door as it shut in her face. She changed into the robe as quickly as she could. Opening the door, she frowned at Gareth, who was standing with his hands casually in his pockets. 'What do you mean "upstairs"?' she queried.

He smiled at her, shrugging. 'What else do you suggest we do? Do you fancy spending the rest of the day wrapped in a Red Cross blanket? I've booked us in here, where we can shower and get something hot to eat.'

She glared suspiciously at him, refusing to budge.

'Have it your way,' he drawled easily. 'But I'm damp and tired and hungry. There's a hot shower and good food in there ... and that's where I'm headed.'

'Wait!' Melissa called. 'I'm coming.'

'I thought you might,' Gareth muttered smugly as he escorted her through the back passage of the hotel to the lift. 'We'll go up this way ... unless of course you want to parade through Reception. There is something rather fetching about a drowned rat in a striped towelling robe.'

'I didn't ask to get like this!' Melissa snapped angrily. 'And just what do you intend to do about my clothes, by the way? And I've no shoes!'

He bundled her into a small lift crowded with trays of fresh linen.

'Ever heard of valet service?' He jabbed

the button and the lift took off. 'Shoes? We'll just have to buy some, won't we? It's not the end of the world, losing a flimsy pair of things like those. The Orientals have the best idea, if you ask me – foot-binding!'

'Well, I'm not asking you!' Melissa snapped, pulling the outsize robe tighter around her. The lift came to a bumpy halt before she was able to remind Gareth that he hadn't been able to keep his eyes off the flimsy things Dian had worn on her feet at the Blue Moon!

'This way!' he called over his shoulder, leaving her to follow. Melissa mumbled under her breath, praying no one would walk out of one of the rooms and have a heart attack at seeing her trailing along.

Gareth stopped halfway along the corridor. 'This is it – the penthouse suite. Enter all those who dare!' he chanted mockingly, unlocking the door and stepping back for her to walk in.

She threw him one of her blackest looks. It was either the room or the Land Rover. She begrudgingly walked in.

She caught her breath, blinking several times at the white and gold décor. Persian rugs lay scattered on the floor and a thick-pile carpet felt like marshmallow under her cold, bare feet. And to complete the effect a magnificent four-poster bed complete with frills stood under a matching canopy.

'It's … lovely…!' she found herself gasping.

'I thought you might change your mind.'

Melissa walked to the window, feeling as though she was in a dream. Was it only two weeks ago she had met this infuriating, frustrating, indescribably annoying man, and was she really standing in a hotel room with him – without her clothes?

'Glastonbury Tor,' Gareth remarked beside her as she focused on a faraway hill broodily overlooking the town. 'Now if you'd brought some sensible clothes with you we might have a decent breath of fresh air climbing to the top!'

Melissa swivelled around, only to be stunned into silence with her heart rebounding under her ribcage as she saw him standing in another robe exactly like hers.

'Snap!' A Cheshire Cat smile spread across his face. 'Now all we've got left to quarrel about is whether you'd like to soap my back first or shall I soap yours … depending of course on whether you bath or shower before I do.'

'You really have had all this worked out, haven't you?' Melissa hissed through clenched teeth, screwing up her eyes. 'You planned it all … every inch of the way! You probably even manufactured the flat tyre!'

His grin broke into a soft chuckle as he came towards her and took her into his arms. 'The flat tyre, I have to say, was an act of God– He does appear to be on my side, you must admit! As for the rain and your heel breaking – not guilty. I had planned something a little more ingenious ... a pleasant lunch, wine, soft background music in the heart of the mystical, magical centre of the esoteric world. The fact that the distributors are only ten minutes away was just a stroke of good luck.'

Gareth's innocent eyes twinkled as he added, 'You did, however, very nearly spoil all my plans by throwing yourself at a six-foot lorry driver.'

Melissa felt the trembling uncertainty of her own body as she refused to relax into the strong arms. 'But why? How can you possibly think of – this – behind Dian's back?'

'Heaven help me, Melissa,' Gareth growled, kissing her neck in soft slow sweeps. 'Don't you know by now? I can't abide the woman! We never had a relation-ship – ever. I'll admit I found her attractive at first ... but I soon discovered Dian only uses people as stepping-stones. She only followed me to England because I'm a fairly safe bet for a meal ticket!'

'But I saw you in the garden with her...'

Gareth's face contorted as he laughed. 'She was trying on the tears when I told her how I felt about you. She wanted to make some idiotic dates for me to go to London with her. I did the gentlemanly thing and offered her a tissue, cross my heart.'

Melissa lifted her eyes to the luminous depths of the green almonds surveying her. 'How you felt ... about me?'

He drew her close, kissing the soft curves of her mouth. 'Don't you know by now, my darling – surely you do? Don't you know how I've felt about you – from the very first minute I ever set eyes on you?'

Melissa shook her head in dumb surprise, hardly able to take in what she was hearing. 'But I'm not in Dian's league ... I only know about animals...'

'And about people and being kind and compassionate and trying to preserve life. Something a person like Dian has no conception of.'

'But she told me...'

'She lied to you because she knew I'd fallen in love with you. She couldn't bear to think someone else had something she couldn't have. The day I met you, Melissa, my whole life changed. Perhaps Dian was the first to recognise that fact. You certainly didn't!'

Melissa ran her fingers over the broad outline of muscular shoulder down the rounded curve of arm which felt so hard under her touch. Could she believe him? Could all he was telling her be true? Or was it just another story made up in order to convince her that the delightful four-poster behind them was a legitimate resting place for the night?

She wanted to believe him so much, she loved him beyond all her wild imaginings. Where did trust begin and suspicion end, when you were in a man's arms, so desperately wanting his truth to be your truth?

'You don't believe me, do you?' Gareth's fingers dug into her arms, jerking her head upwards so that she had to look into the serious eyes.

'I didn't think there was such a thing as love at first sight,' Melissa said stubbornly.

'Nor did I,' Gareth agreed in a brittle voice, 'until I met you. But, try as I might to encourage you to discuss the subject with me, I seem fated to get no response.'

She raised her lowered lids. 'But those letters ... the ones Dian accused me of writing?'

Gareth sighed, the firm chest easing itself into her tightening breasts as she waited expectantly for the answer. 'Dian jumped to the conclusion that the name Lissa was short for Melissa. Lissa Forbes was like a kid sister to me. Except that she developed a childish romantic notion after getting herself mixed up in some sort of commune. Realising it was all pie in the sky, she kept writing to ask me if she could come out to Australia. I don't have to tell you what my answer was, do I? Ask Walter if you don't believe me – Lissa is his daughter.'

Melissa felt a pang of relief flood through her, remembering Walter's account of his wayward daughter which Gareth certainly couldn't have known he'd divulged.

Gareth's smile widened, the white teeth making her heart somersault as he admitted ruefully, 'I have to say Dian's jumping to the wrong conclusion about the letters rather appealed to me. I thought it couldn't do any harm to let her go on thinking that, and it might just make you a little more jealous...'

Melissa groaned softly. 'Jealous! If only you knew ... when I saw you and Dian together at the Blue Moon...'

'What about you and Peter?' Gareth quickly defended. 'I realised he was beginning to fall for you ... in a big way. Given enough time, the chances were I'd lose you. What else could I do?'

Melissa traced a dark strand of hair across his forehead, loving every inch of him. 'Your plan succeeded,' she confessed softly. 'I was about to give you a piece of my mind that night you all trooped in like the Three Musketeers!'

Gareth laughed deeply, holding her so closely she could hardly breathe. 'But you kept quiet?'

'Only because I fell asleep!'

'And to think I prowled around in my

251

room waiting for you to come in and call me all the names under the sun!'

'What would you have done if I had?' Melissa asked teasingly, linking her arms around his strong neck and running her hands through damp, thick hair.

'I would have done this...' Gareth swept her off her feet and carried her to the four-poster, falling with her into the deep folds of the bed.

Her grey eyes were teasing and restless as he gazed down into them, his large hands cupping the bright cloud of golden hair which fanned out across the pillow.

'So ... where do we go from here?' he asked, covering the pale lips that trembled under his touch.

Melissa sighed. 'I've no clothes, no shoes, I'm extremely dirty and I'm ravenously hungry ... and we still have a certain vehicle to collect.' Feeling a hand at the nape of her neck tilting her head upwards to be kissed, she parted her lips expectantly.

'What would you say,' came the deep voice, and then a soft, butterfly kiss, 'if we put off all the things we ought to be doing and concentrated on just one?'

She raised dainty fair eyebrows to enquire, 'And what would that be?'

She could hardly catch her breath as with heart-piercing delight she saw the wide mouth form the words, 'I ... love ... you.'

'You do?'

Gareth grinned devilishly. 'In your – er – sensible planning for the future, would there be room for a tallish, darkish man, hard-working, reliable and good at tyre-changing, to look after you and your three or four smallish, darkish…?'

'Dogs?' Melissa asked with rising laughter in her voice.

Gareth shook his head, planting a kiss on the freckled nose.

'Cats?' she squealed as he pulled her slender body to roll on top of him.

He kissed the teasing lips, too long and too intensely for her to enquire about sheep or pigs.

Some time later, when Melissa lay in paradise, Gareth was to describe to her the brood of Tremaines which, far from being animals, in a very short number of years would be called by Mrs Carter 'angels with the dirtiest faces on God's green earth.'

This Large Print Book, for people
who cannot read normal print,
is published under the auspices of

THE ULVERSCROFT FOUNDATION